HERE'S HEATHCLIFF by Geo Gately

AMERICA'S
CRAZIEST
CAT!

Volume V

© McNaught Synd., Inc.

THE BEST OF SUNDAY WITH HEATHCLIFF

HEATHCLIFF

THE BEST OF FRIENDS

TOR

A TOM DOHERTY ASSOCIATES BOOK

This is a work of fiction. All the characters and events portrayed in this book are fictional, and any resemblance to real people or incidents is purely coincidental.

HEATHCLIFF: THE BEST OF FRIENDS
Volume V of HERE'S HEATHCLIFF

Copyright © 1981 by McNaught Syndicate, Inc.

All rights reserved, including the right to reproduce this book or portions thereof in any form.

Reprinted by arrangement with Windmill Books, Inc. and Simon and Schuster, a division of Gulf and Western Corp.

First Tor printing: August 1986

A TOR Book

Published by Tom Doherty Associates, Inc.
49 West 24 Street
New York, N.Y. 10010

ISBN: 0-812-56808-7
CAN. ED.: 0-812-56809-5

Printed in the United States of America

0 9 8 7 6 5 4 3 2 1

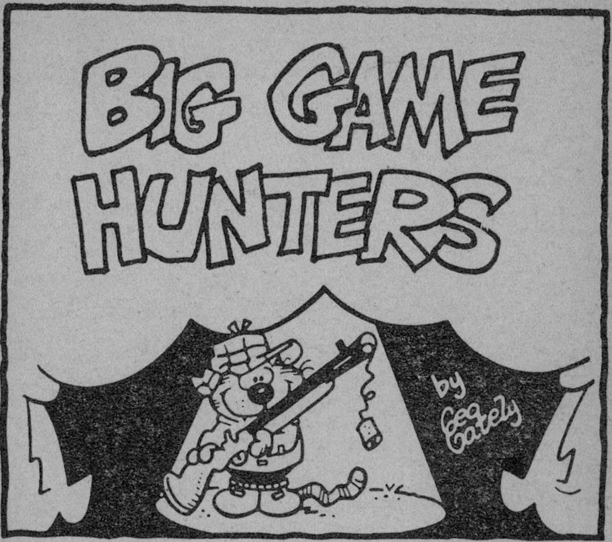
BIG GAME HUNTERS
by Geo Gately

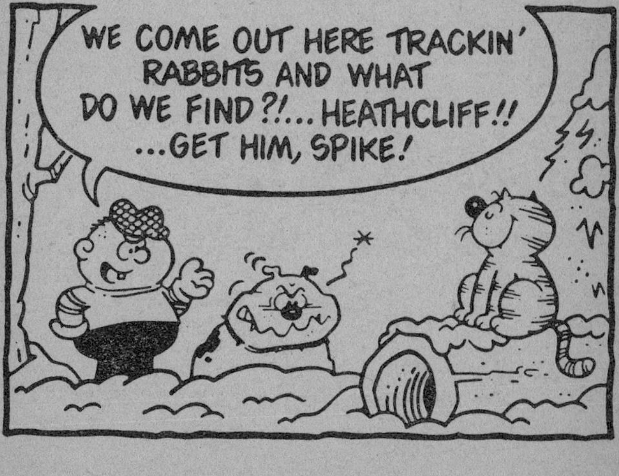
WE COME OUT HERE TRACKIN' RABBITS AND WHAT DO WE FIND?!... HEATHCLIFF!! ...GET HIM, SPIKE!

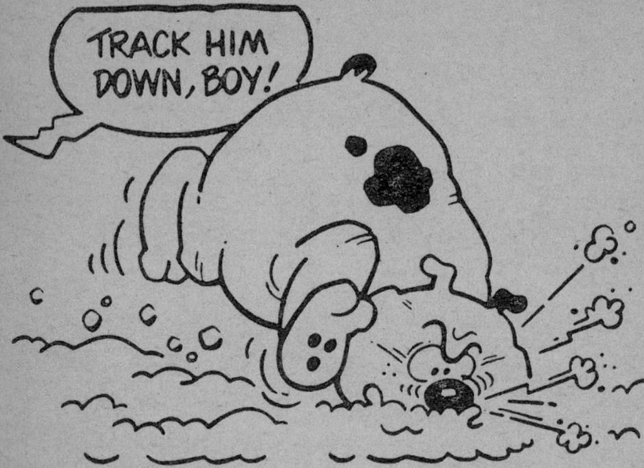
TRACK HIM DOWN, BOY!

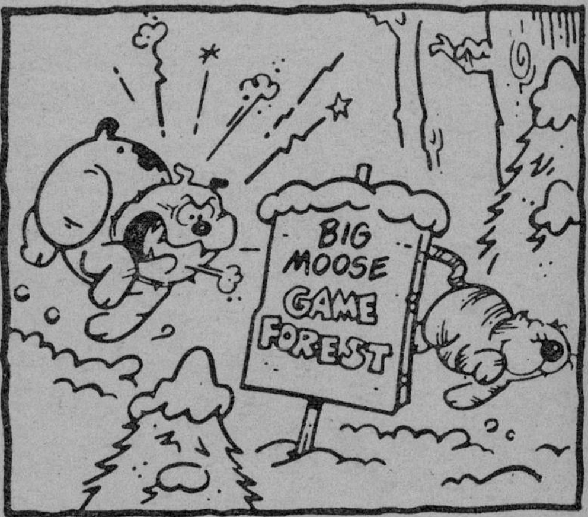
BIG MOOSE GAME FOREST

MOOSE-CALL HORN
SNAP

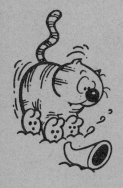

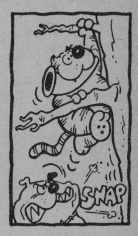

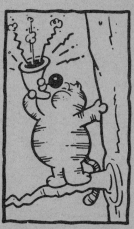

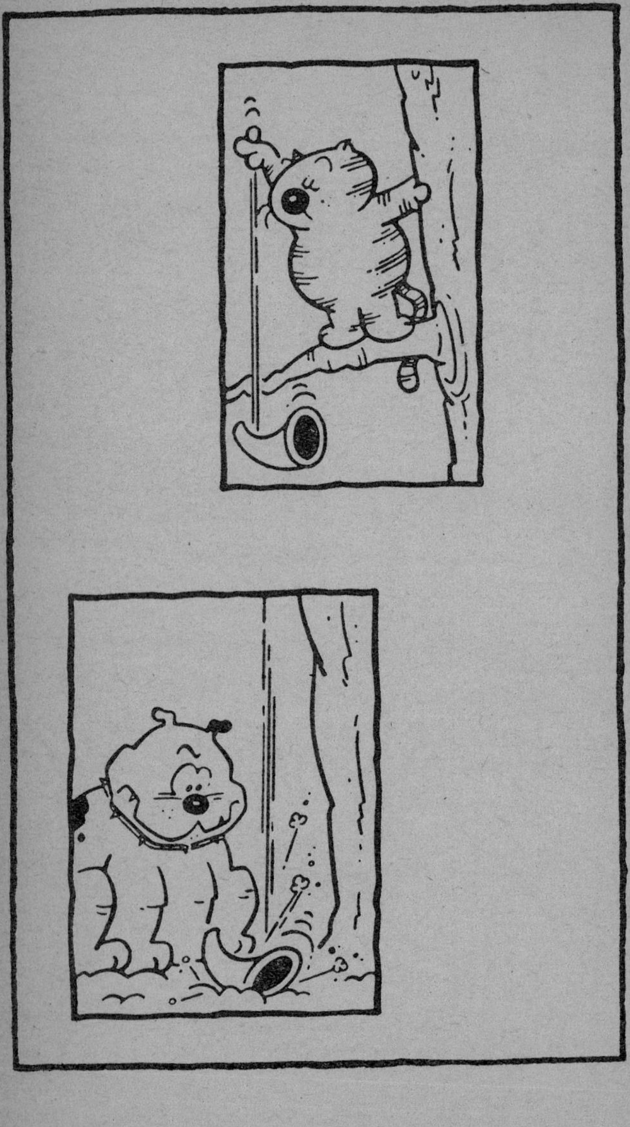

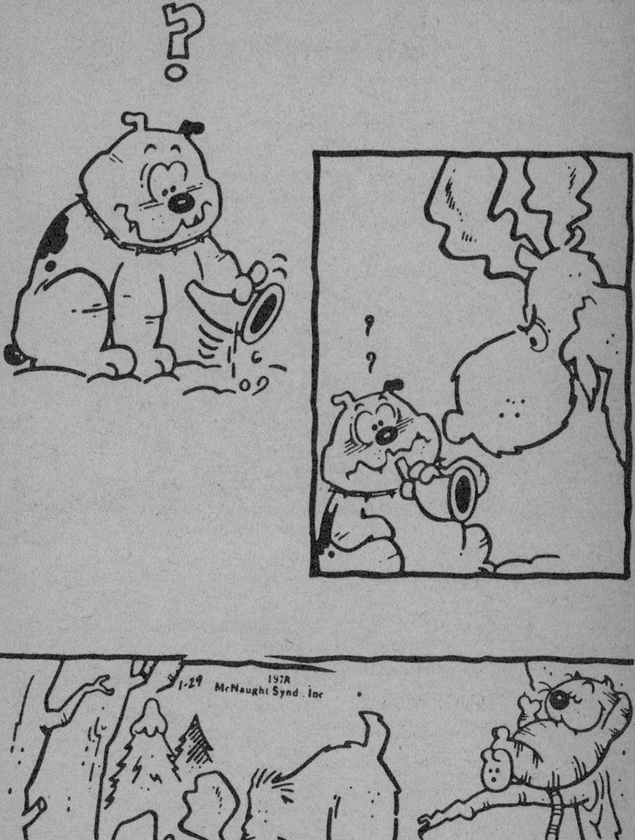
?
? ?
1-29 1978 McNaught Synd. Inc

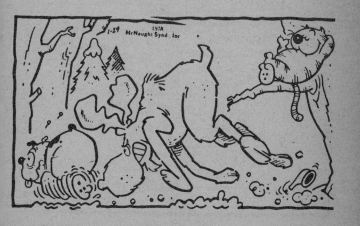

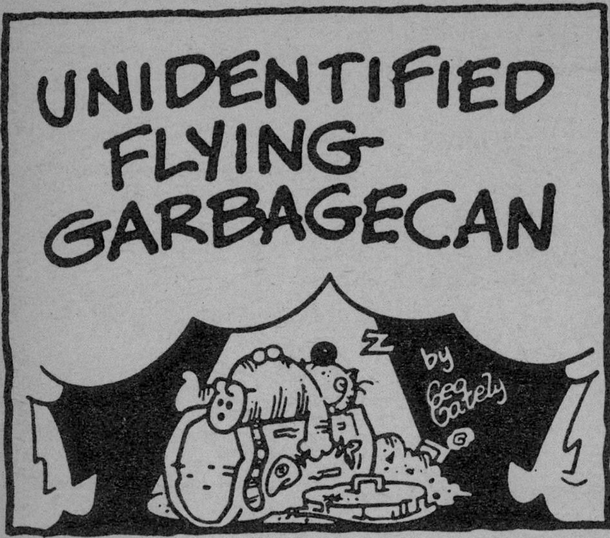
UNIDENTIFIED FLYING GARBAGECAN
Z
by Geo Gately

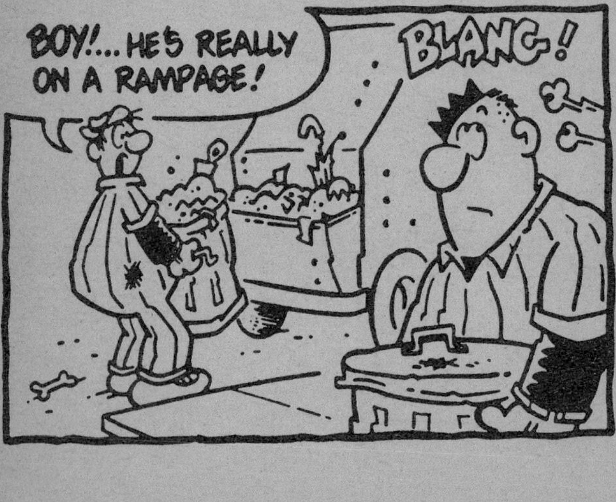
BOY!... HE'S REALLY ON A RAMPAGE!
BLANG!

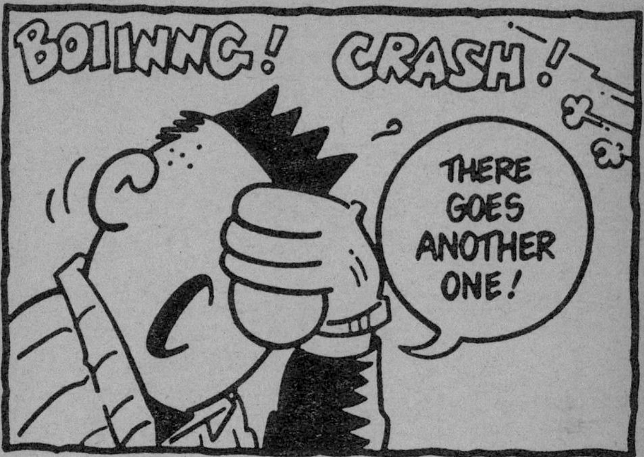
BOIINNG! CRASH!
THERE GOES ANOTHER ONE!

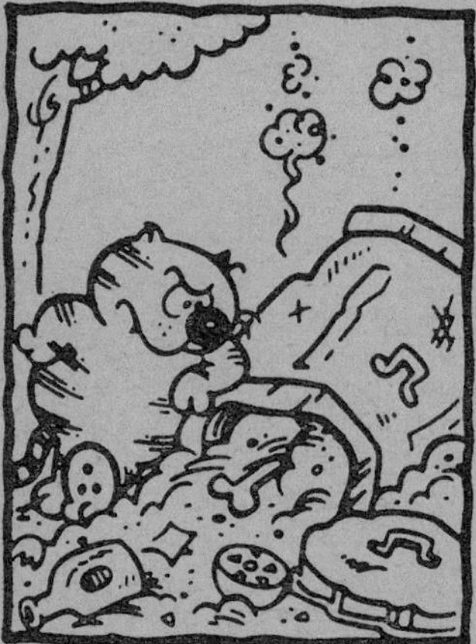

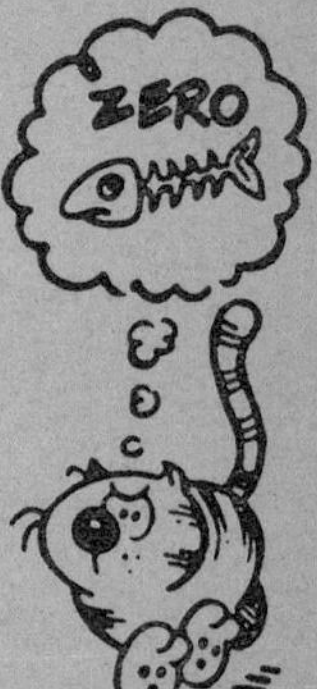
ZERO

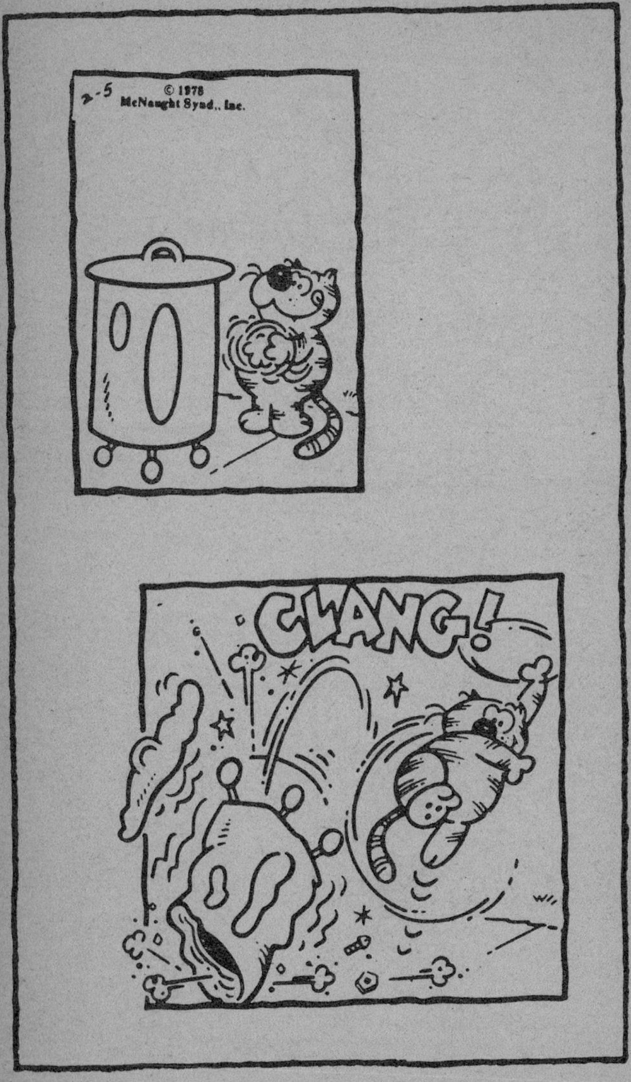
2-5
© 1978
McNaught Synd., Inc.
CLANG!

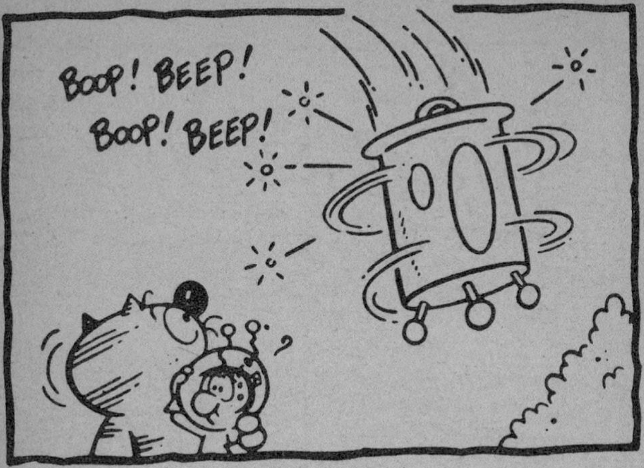
BOOP! BEEP!
BOOP! BEEP!

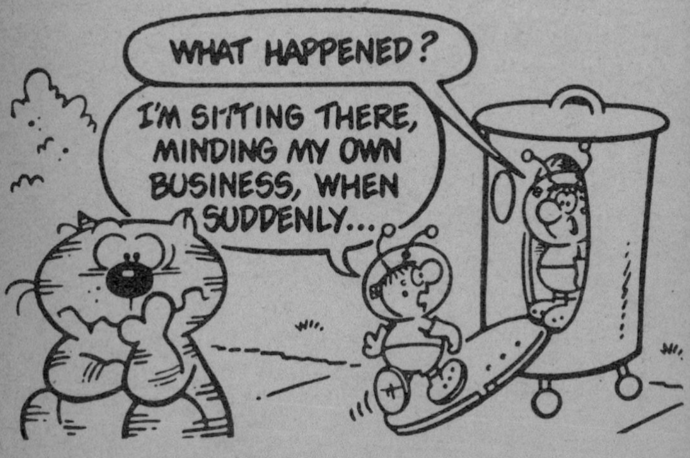
WHAT HAPPENED?
I'M SITTING THERE, MINDING MY OWN BUSINESS, WHEN SUDDENLY...

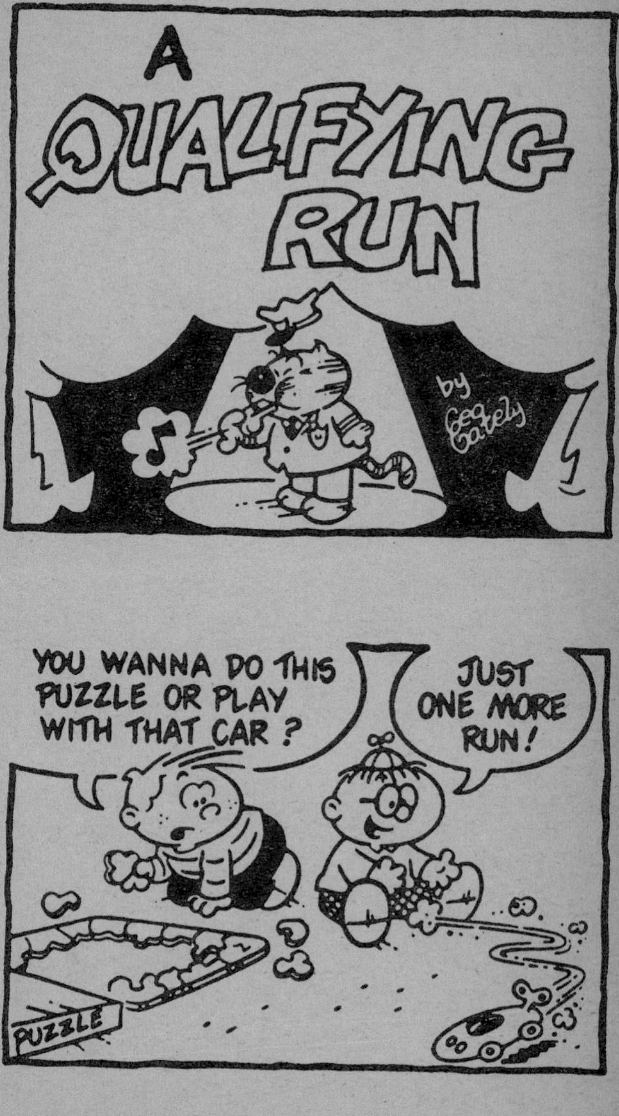
A QUALIFYING RUN
by Geo Gately
YOU WANNA DO THIS PUZZLE OR PLAY WITH THAT CAR ?
JUST ONE MORE RUN!
PUZZLE

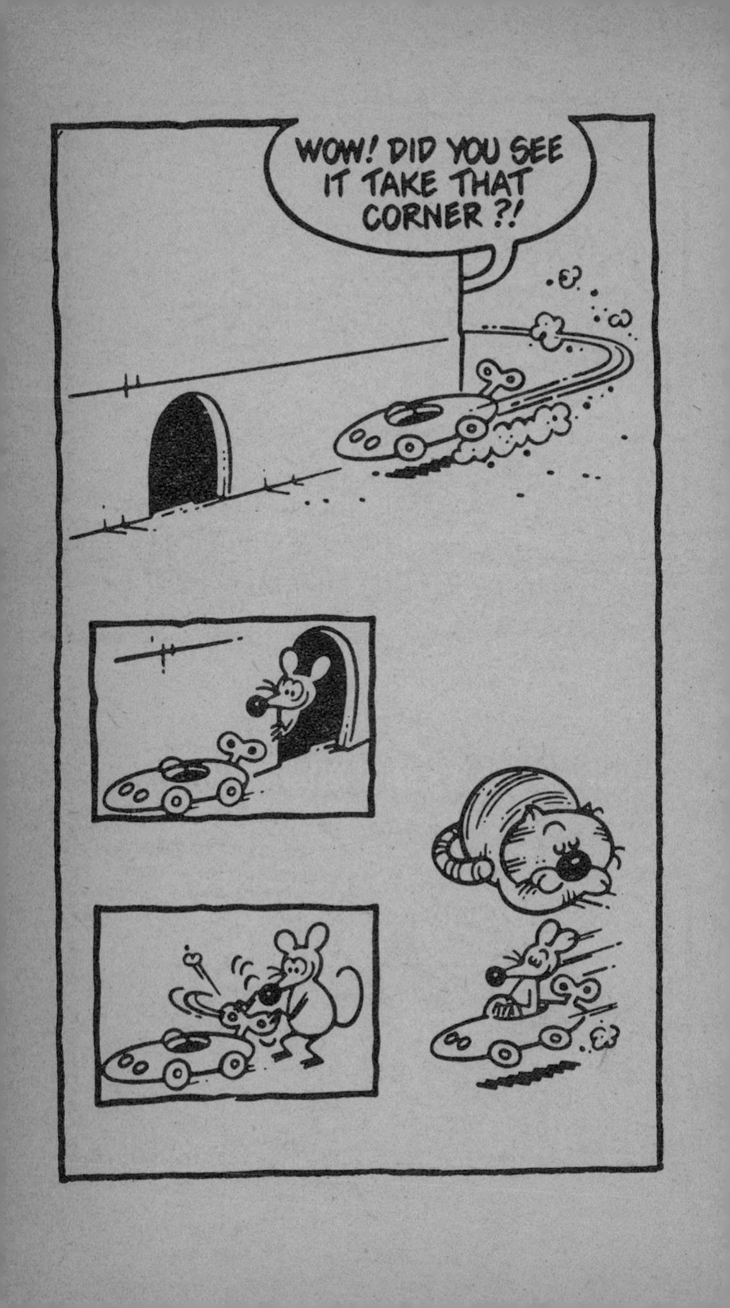
WOW! DID YOU SEE IT TAKE THAT CORNER ?!

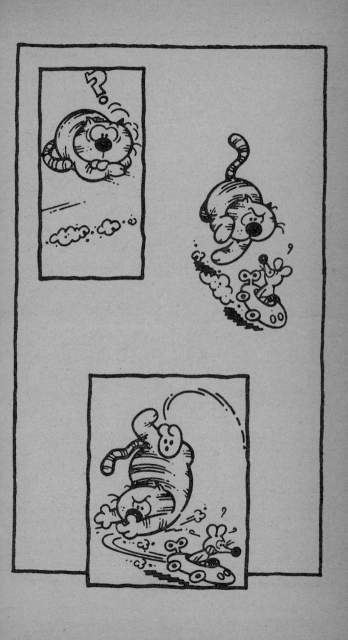

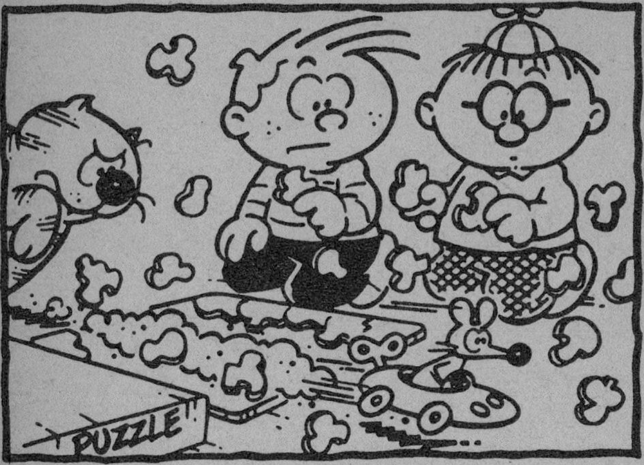
PUZZLE

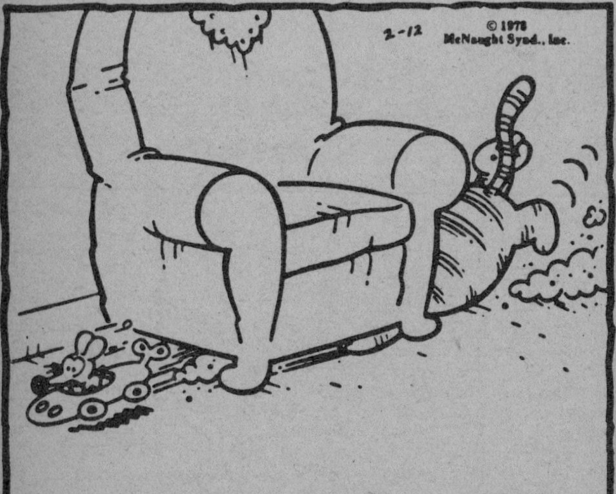
2-12
© 1978
McNaught Synd., Inc.

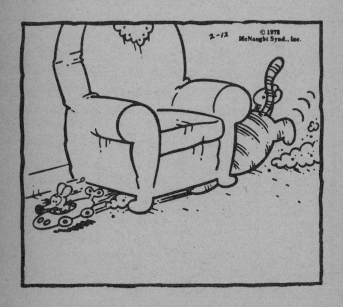

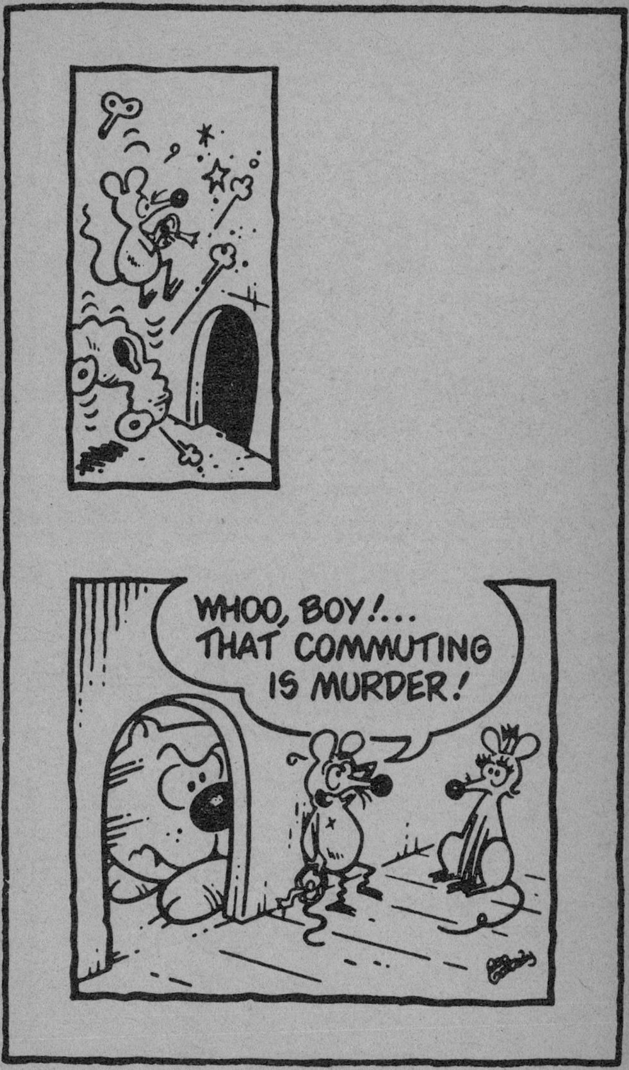
WHOO, BOY!... THAT COMMUTING IS MURDER!

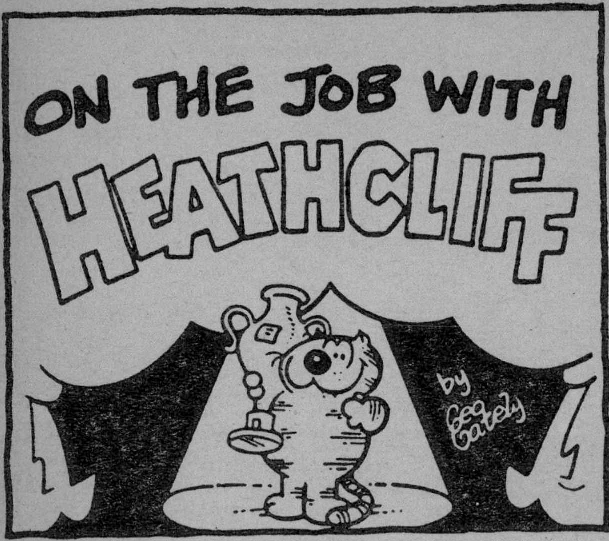
ON THE JOB WITH
HEATHCLIFF
by

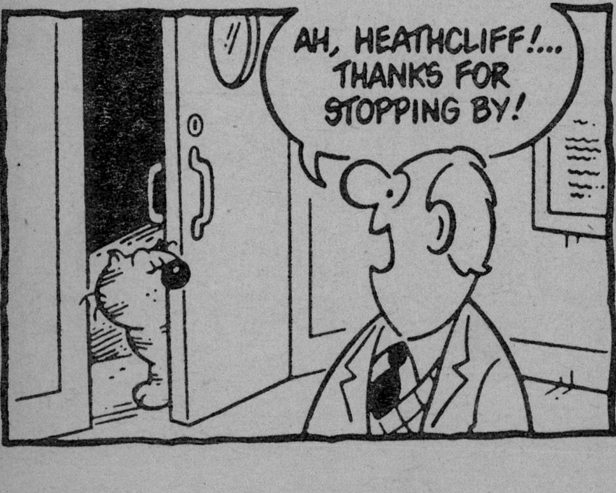
AH, HEATHCLIFF!... THANKS FOR STOPPING BY!

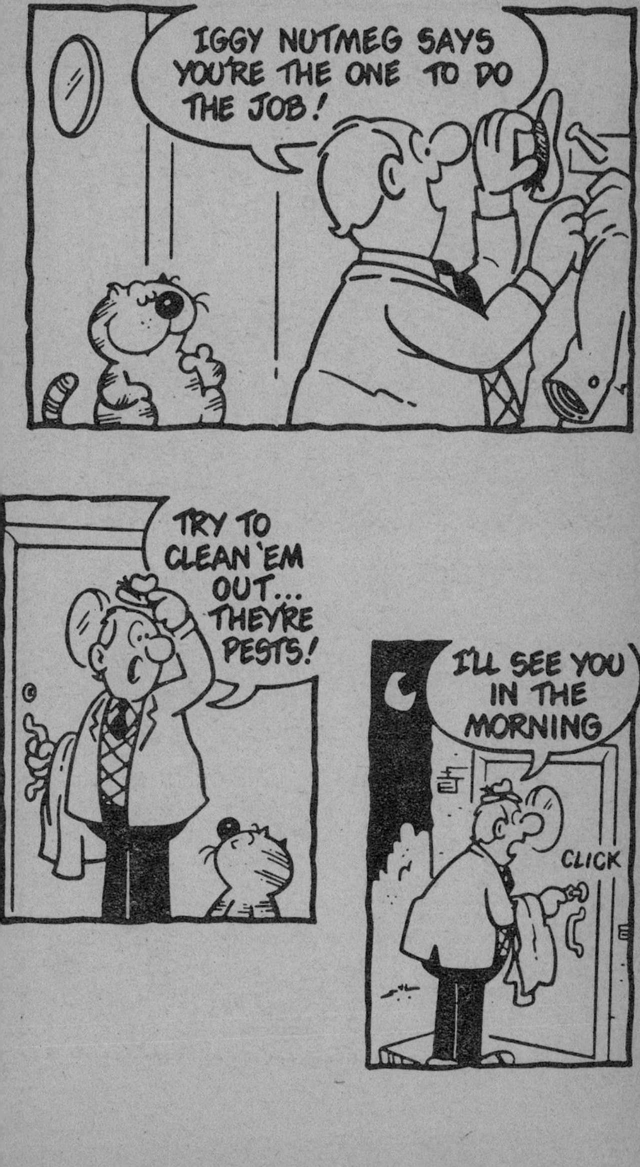
IGGY NUTMEG SAYS YOU'RE THE ONE TO DO THE JOB!
TRY TO CLEAN 'EM OUT... THEY'RE PESTS!
I'LL SEE YOU IN THE MORNING
CLICK

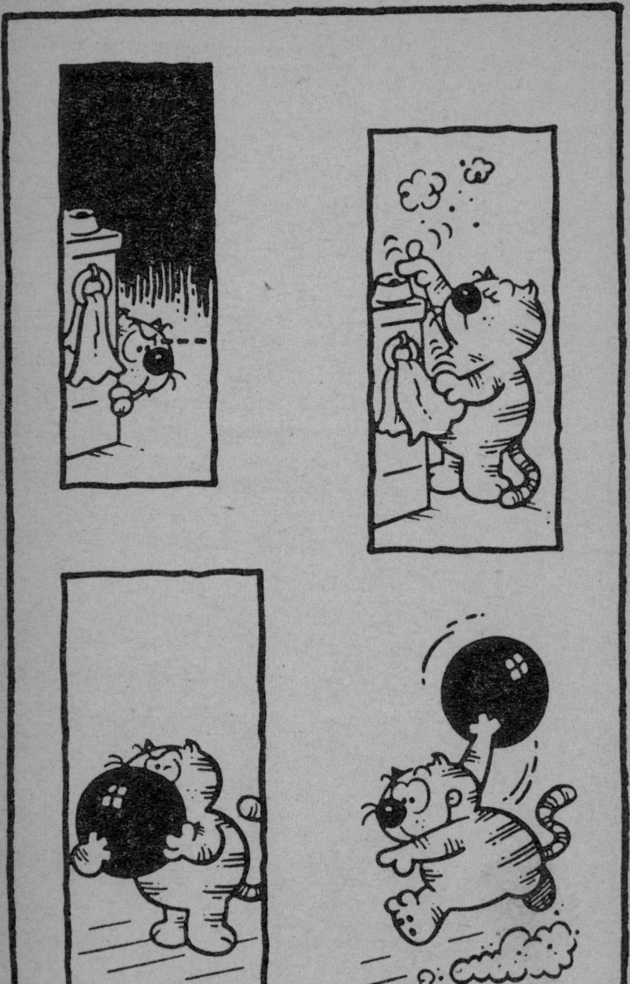

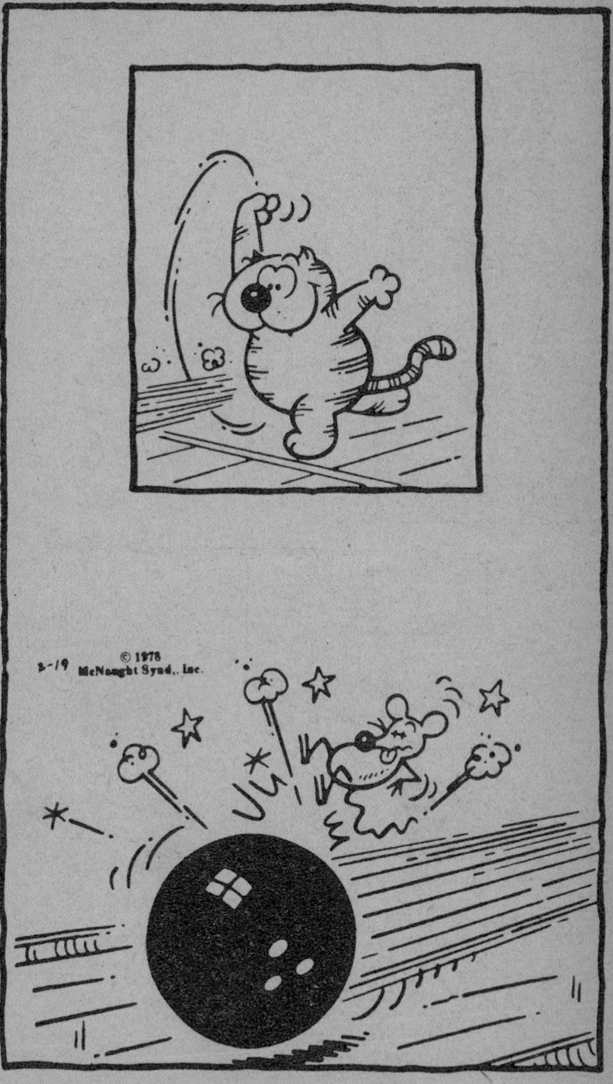

2-19 © 1978 McNaught Synd., Inc.

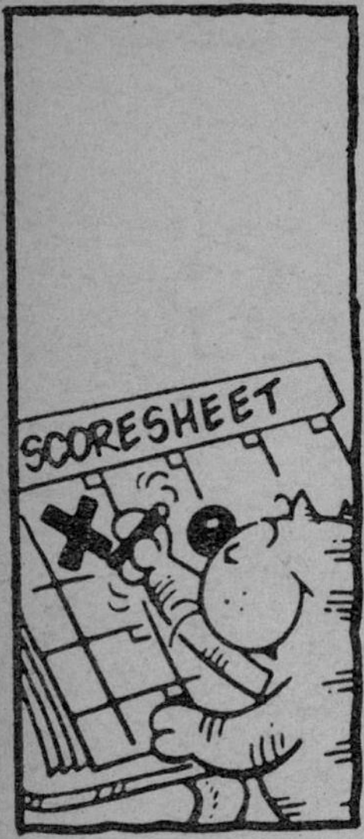
SCORESHEET

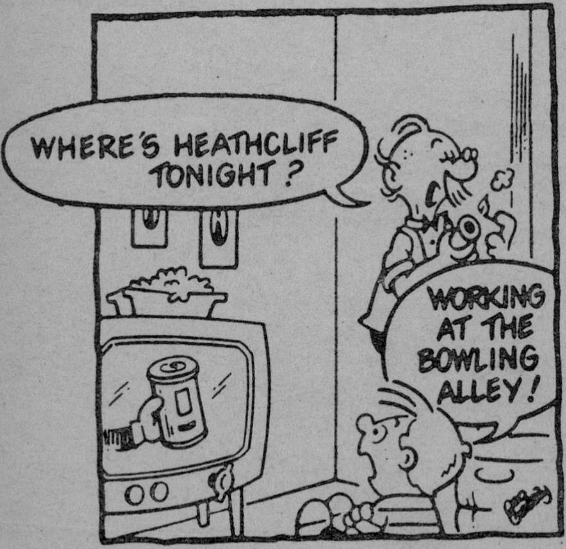
WHERE'S HEATHCLIFF TONIGHT?
WORKING AT THE BOWLING ALLEY!

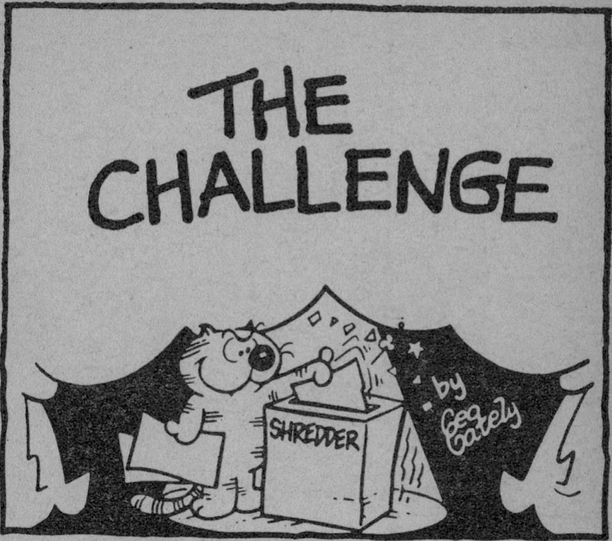
THE CHALLENGE
SHREDDER
by
Geo Gately

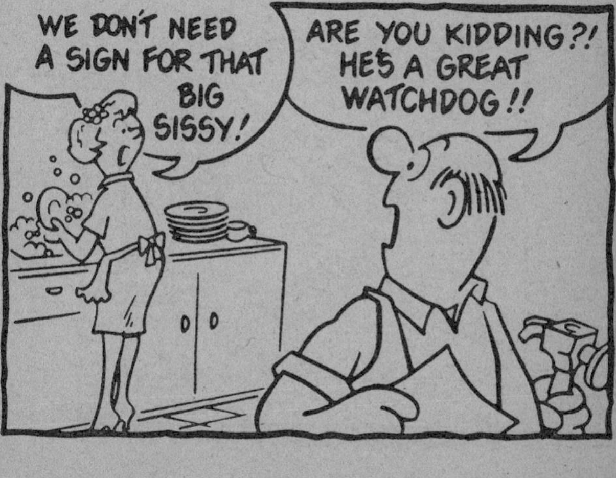
WE DON'T NEED A SIGN FOR THAT BIG SISSY!
ARE YOU KIDDING?! HE'S A GREAT WATCHDOG!!

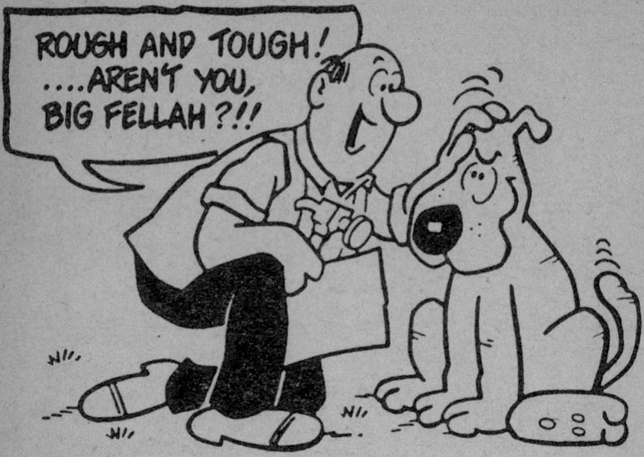
ROUGH AND TOUGH! ....AREN'T YOU, BIG FELLAH ?!!

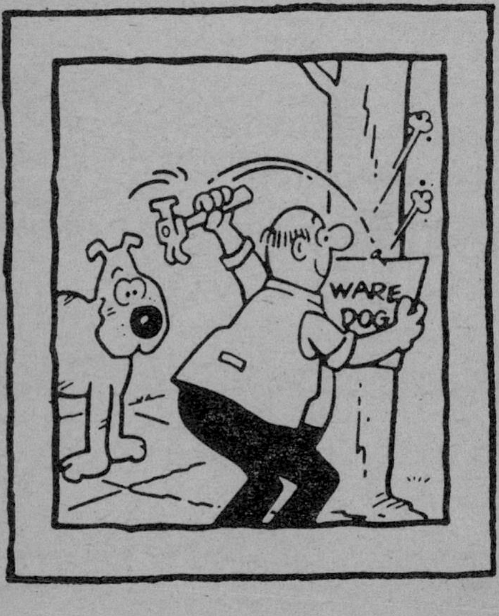
WARE DOG

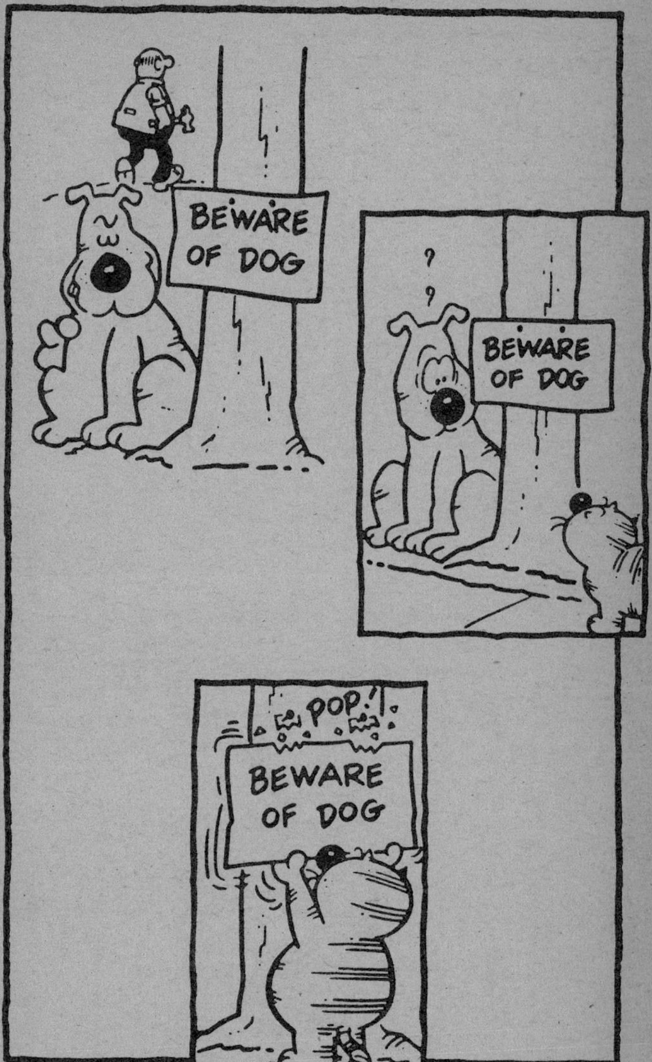
BEWARE OF DOG
BEWARE OF DOG
? ?
POP!
BEWARE OF DOG

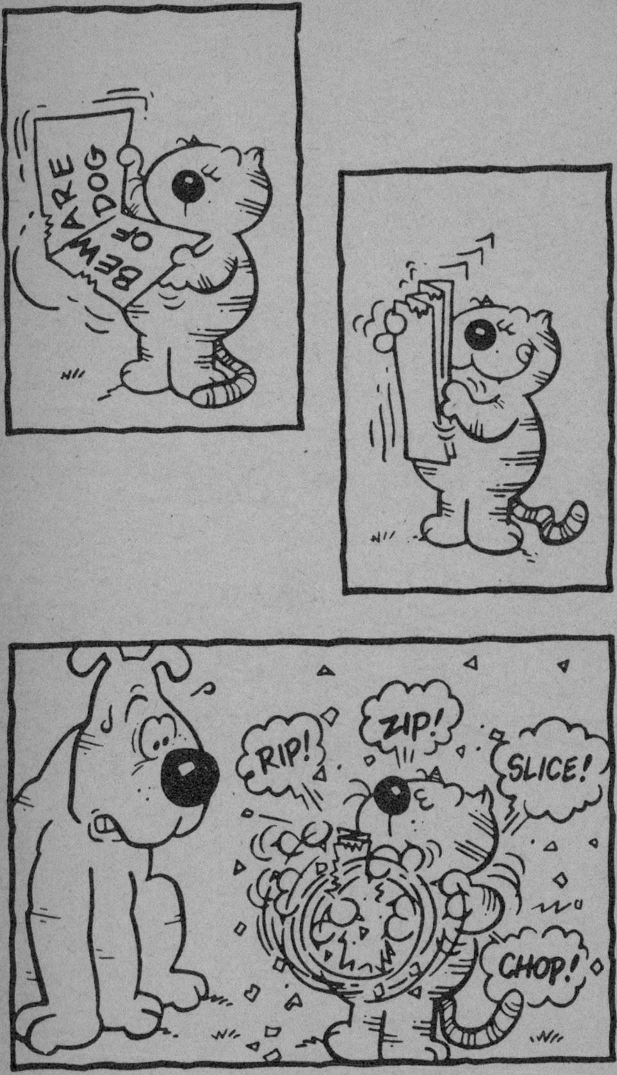
BEWARE OF DOG
RIP!
ZIP!
SLICE!
CHOP!

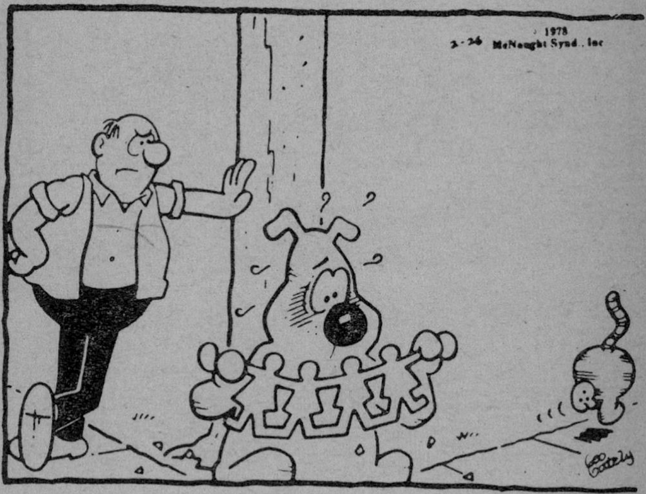

© 1978
2-26 McNaught Synd., Inc

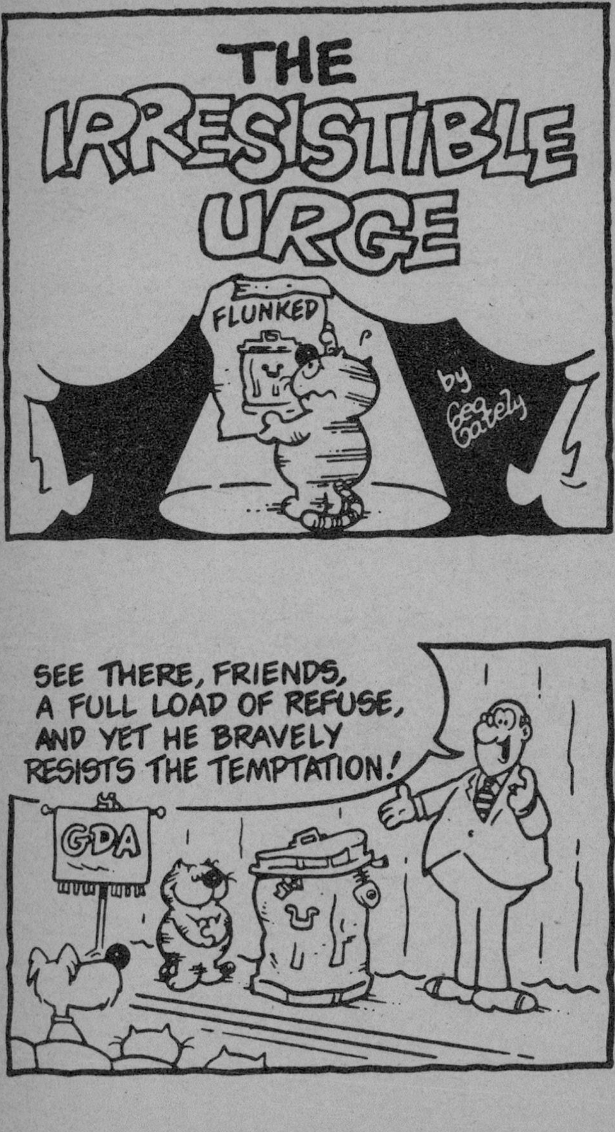
THE IRRESISTIBLE URGE
FLUNKED
by Geo Gately
SEE THERE, FRIENDS, A FULL LOAD OF REFUSE, AND YET HE BRAVELY RESISTS THE TEMPTATION!
GDA

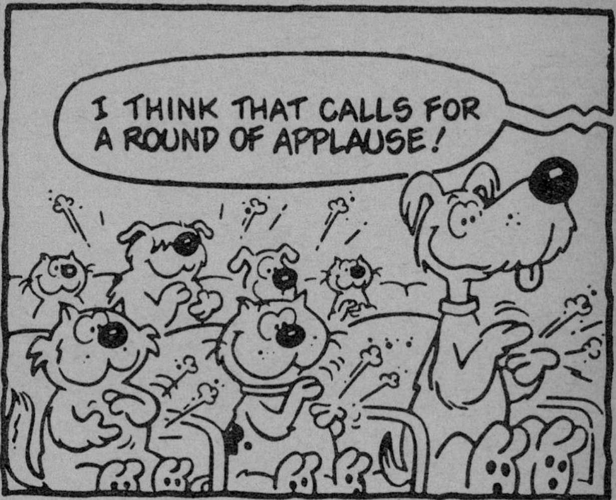
I THINK THAT CALLS FOR A ROUND OF APPLAUSE!

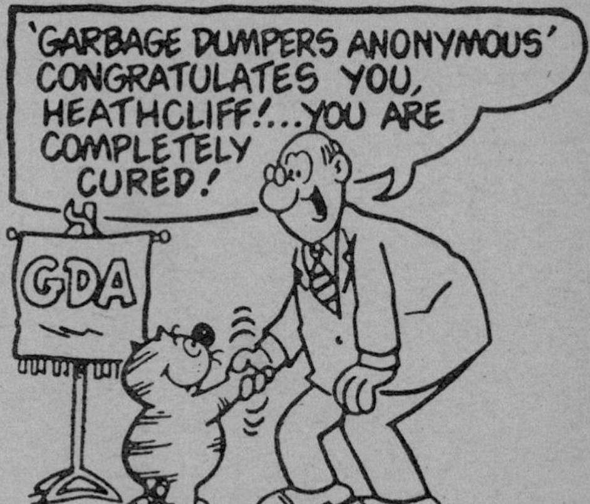
'GARBAGE DUMPERS ANONYMOUS' CONGRATULATES YOU, HEATHCLIFF!...YOU ARE COMPLETELY CURED!
GDA

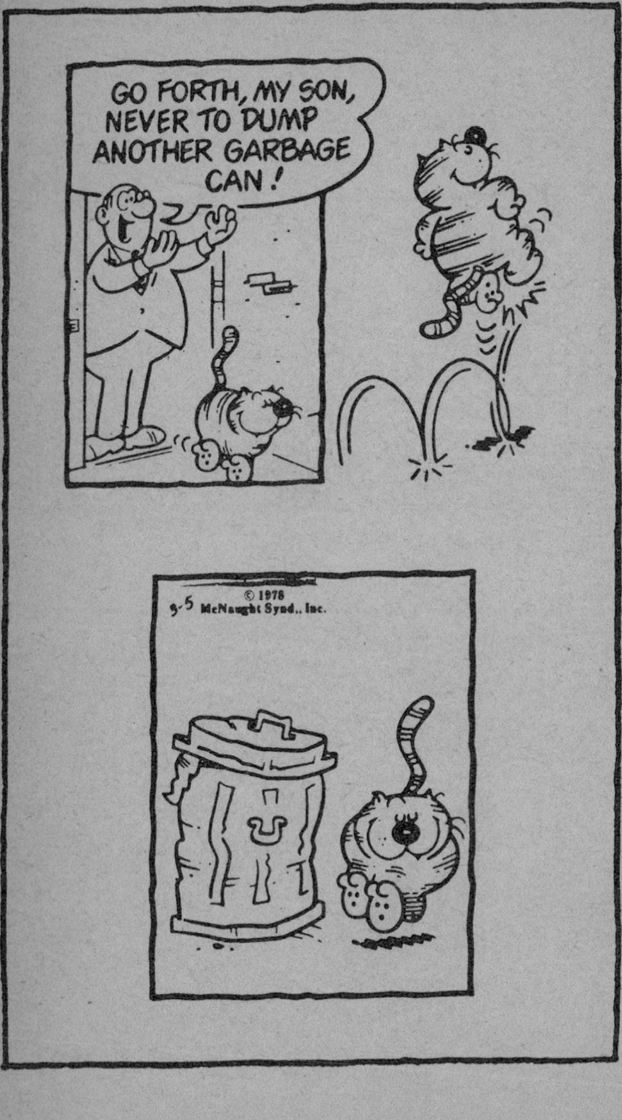
GO FORTH, MY SON, NEVER TO DUMP ANOTHER GARBAGE CAN!
9-5
© 1978 McNaught Synd., Inc.

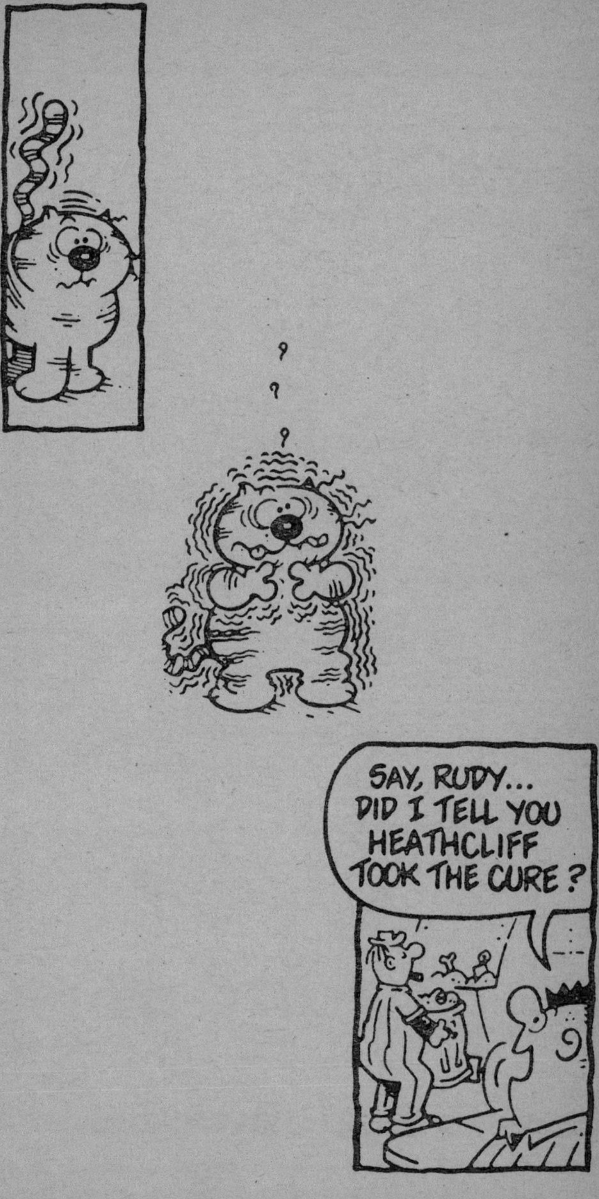
SAY, RUDY... DID I TELL YOU HEATHCLIFF TOOK THE CURE?

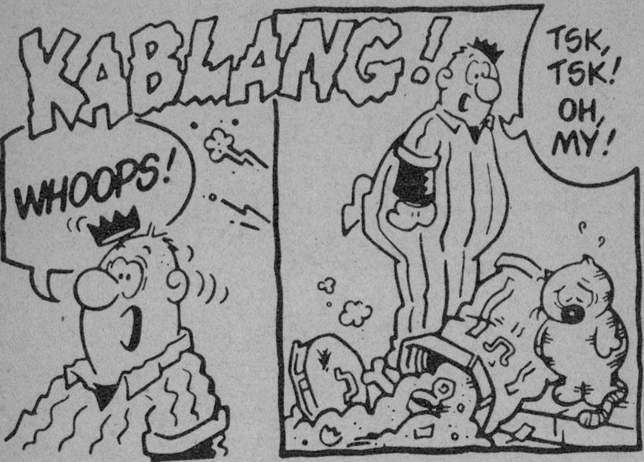
KABLANG!
WHOOPS!
TSK, TSK! OH, MY!

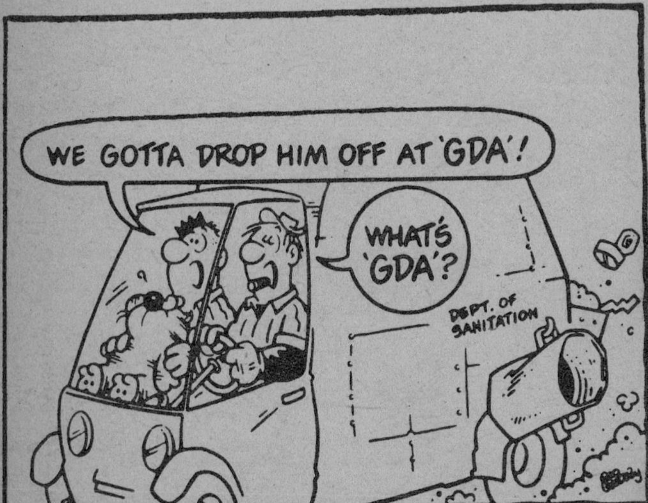
WE GOTTA DROP HIM OFF AT 'GDA'!
WHAT'S 'GDA'?
DEPT. OF SANITATION

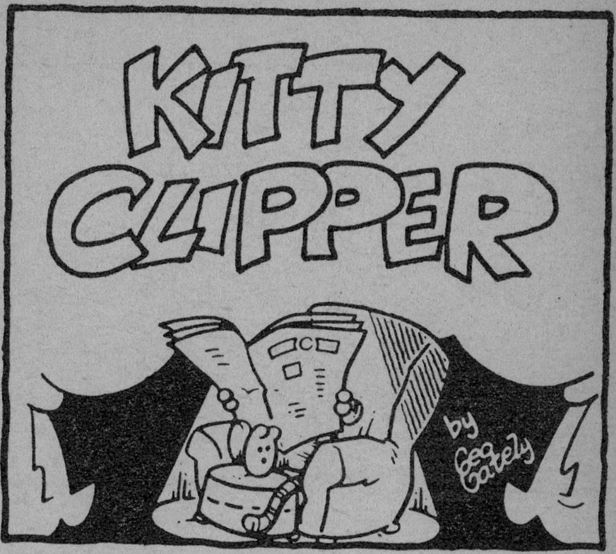
KITTY CLIPPER
by Geo Gately

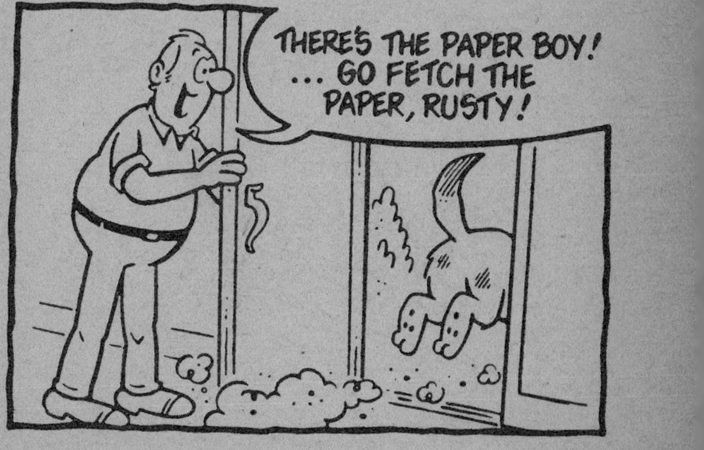
THERE'S THE PAPER BOY! ... GO FETCH THE PAPER, RUSTY!

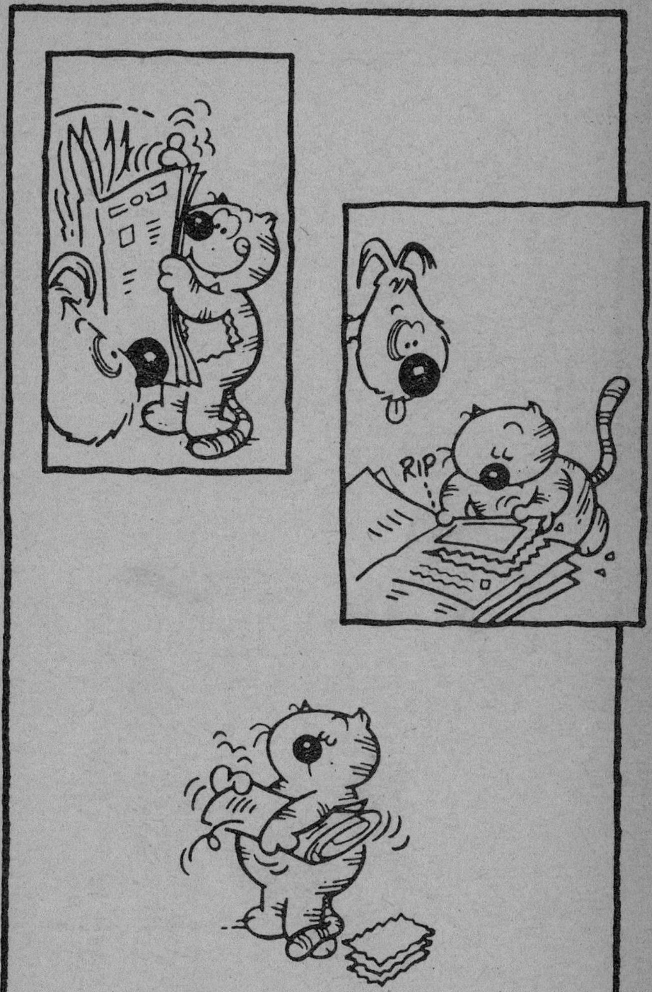
RIP

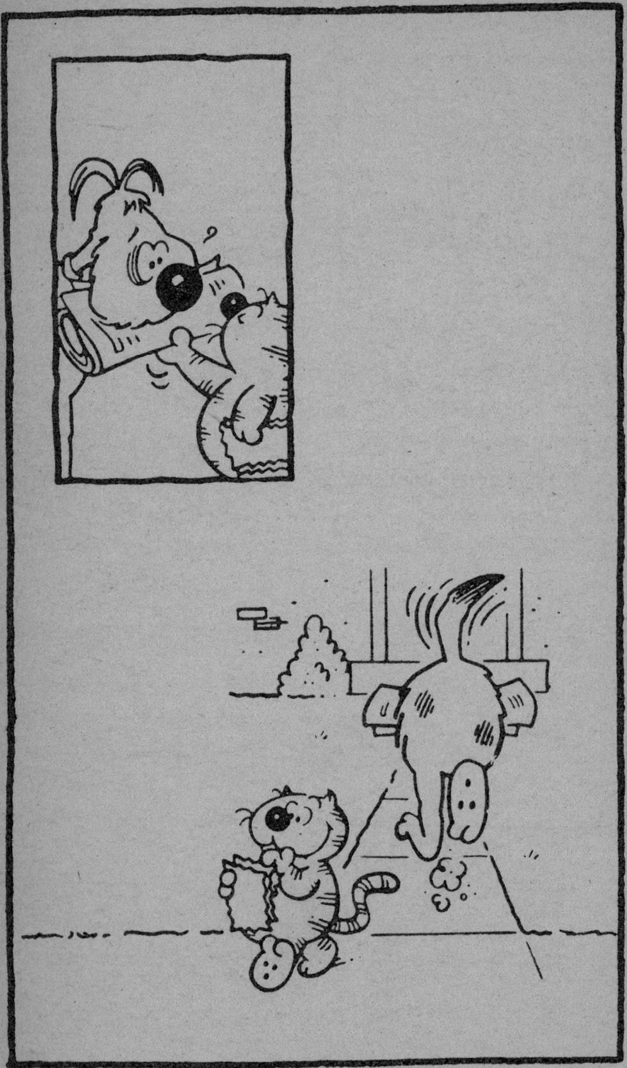

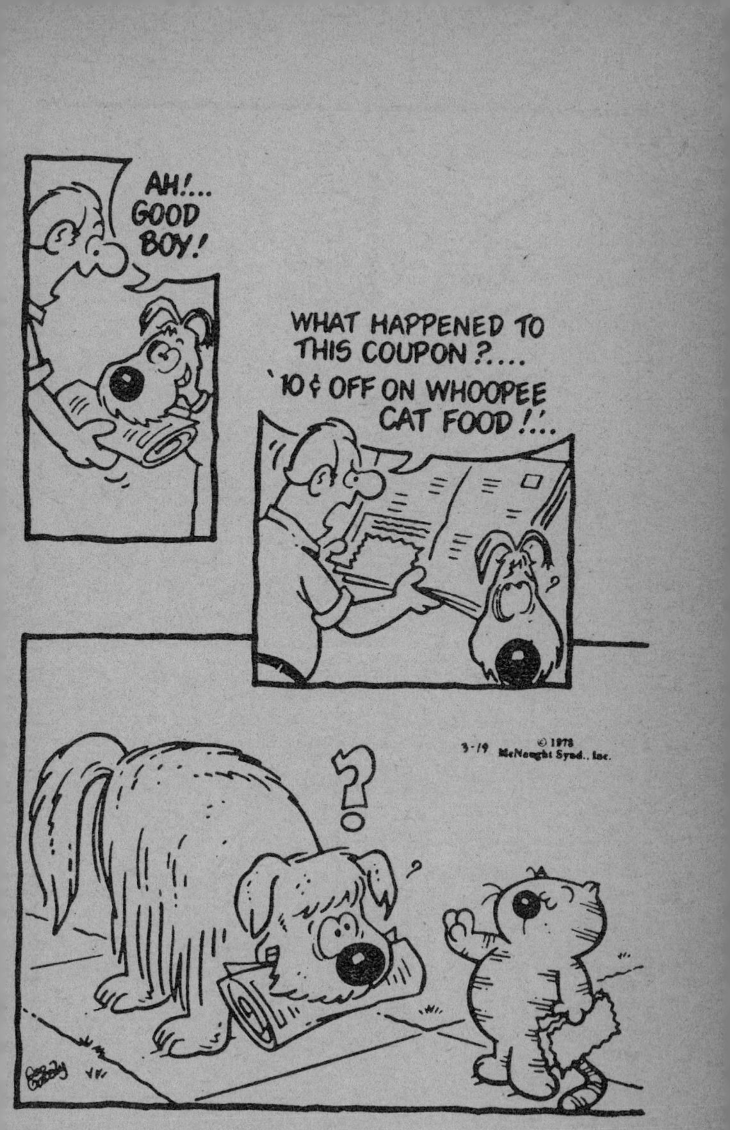
AH!... GOOD BOY!
WHAT HAPPENED TO THIS COUPON ?.... '10¢ OFF ON WHOOPEE CAT FOOD!'...
?
?
?
3-19
© 1978 McNaught Synd., Inc.

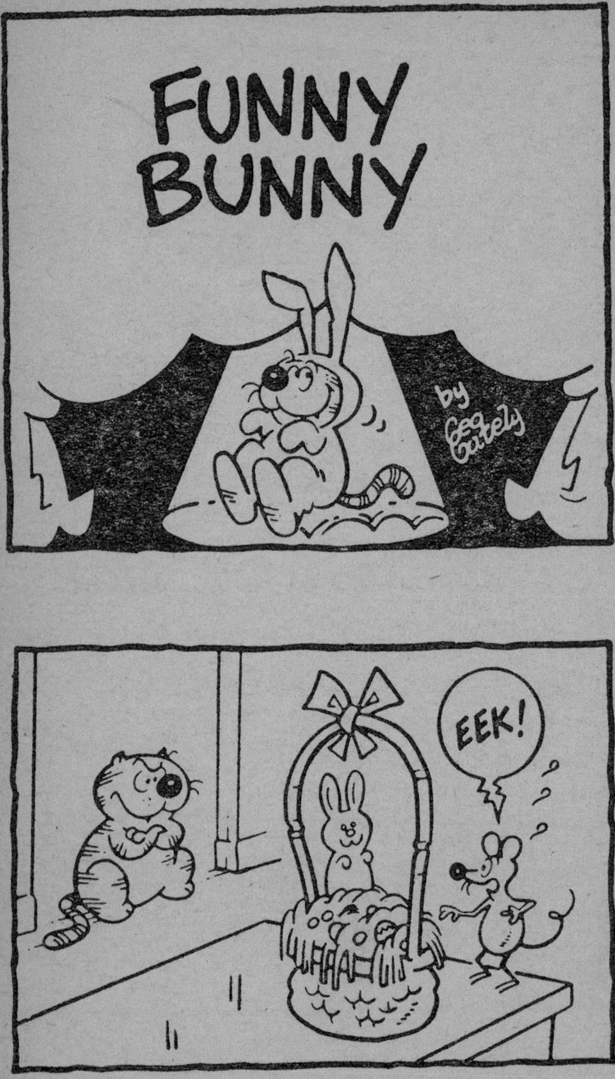
FUNNY BUNNY
by Geo Gately
EEK!

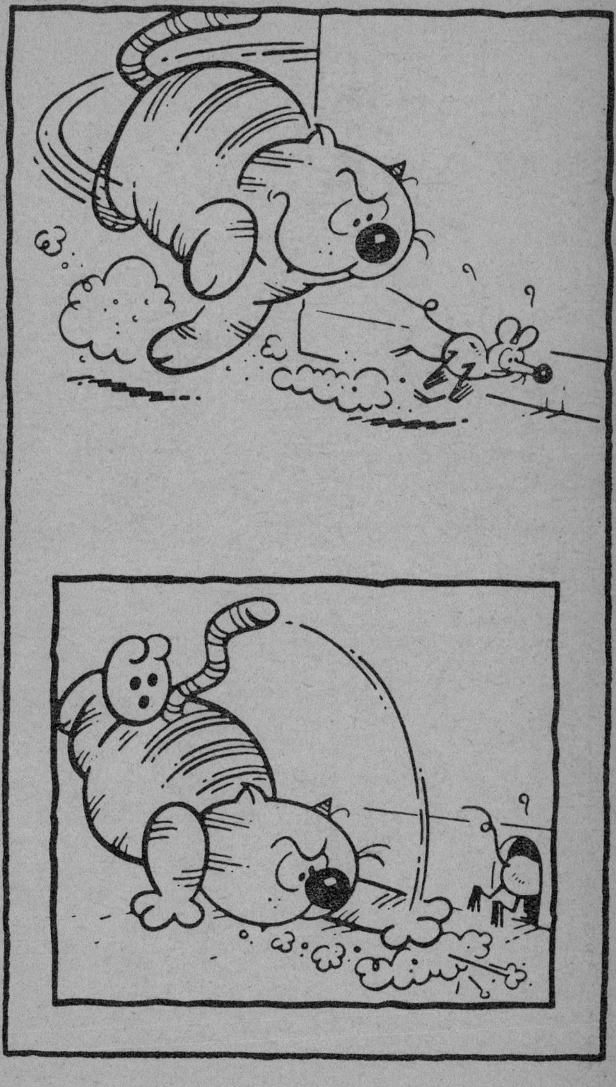

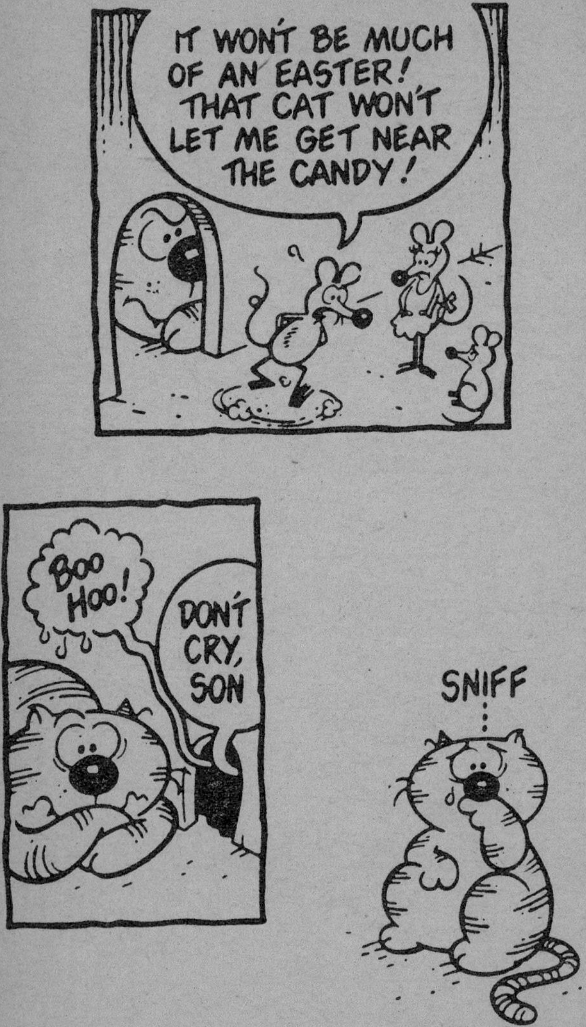
IT WON'T BE MUCH OF AN EASTER! THAT CAT WON'T LET ME GET NEAR THE CANDY!
BOO HOO!
DON'T CRY, SON
SNIFF

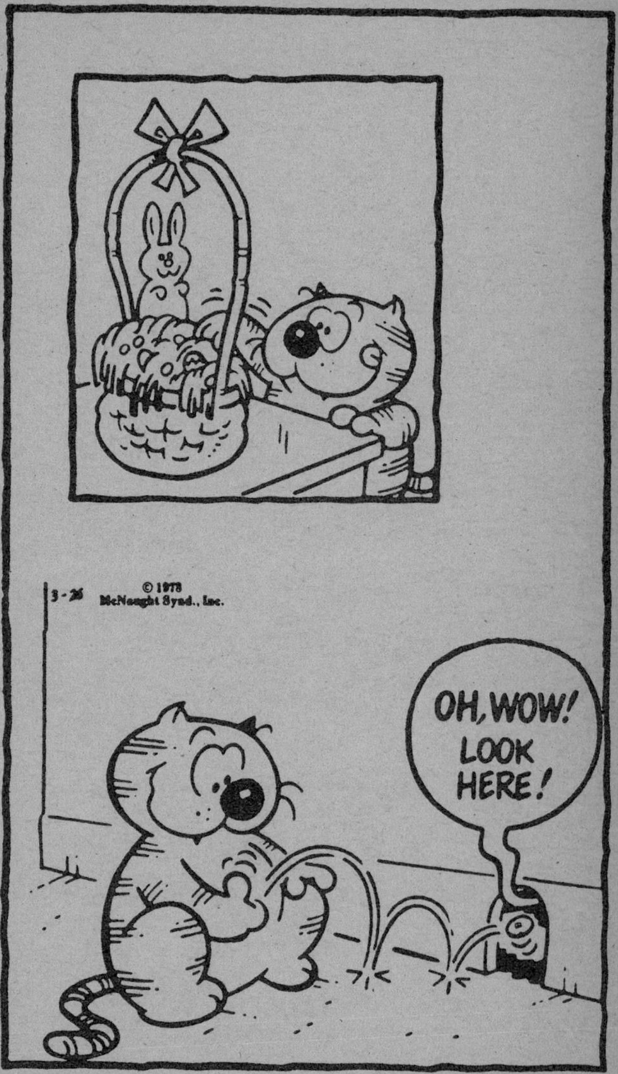
3-26
© 1978
McNaught Synd., Inc.
OH, WOW! LOOK HERE!

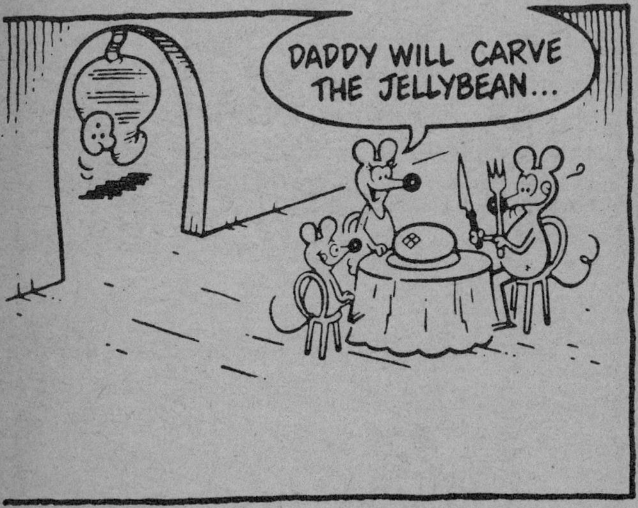
DADDY WILL CARVE THE JELLYBEAN...

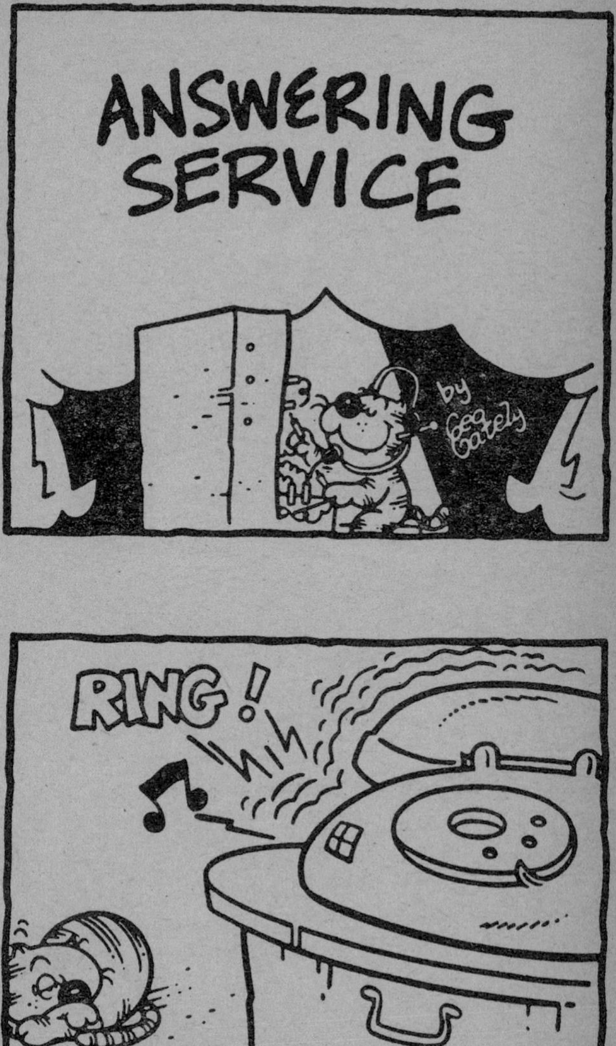
ANSWERING SERVICE
by Leo Lately
RING!

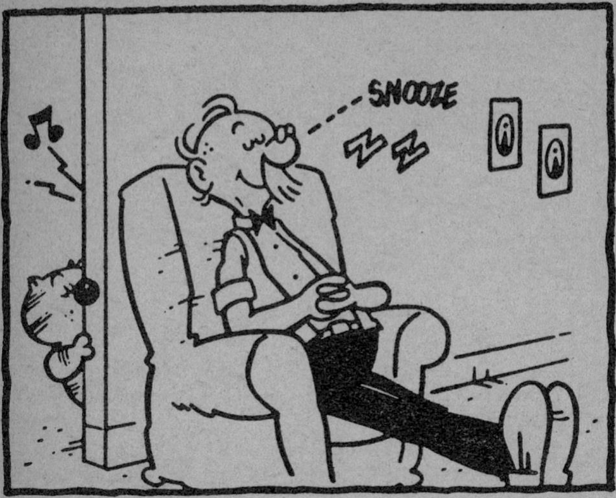
SNOOZE
Z Z

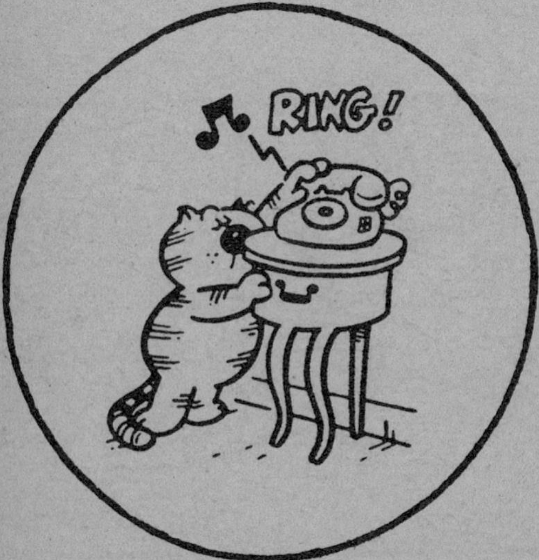
RING!

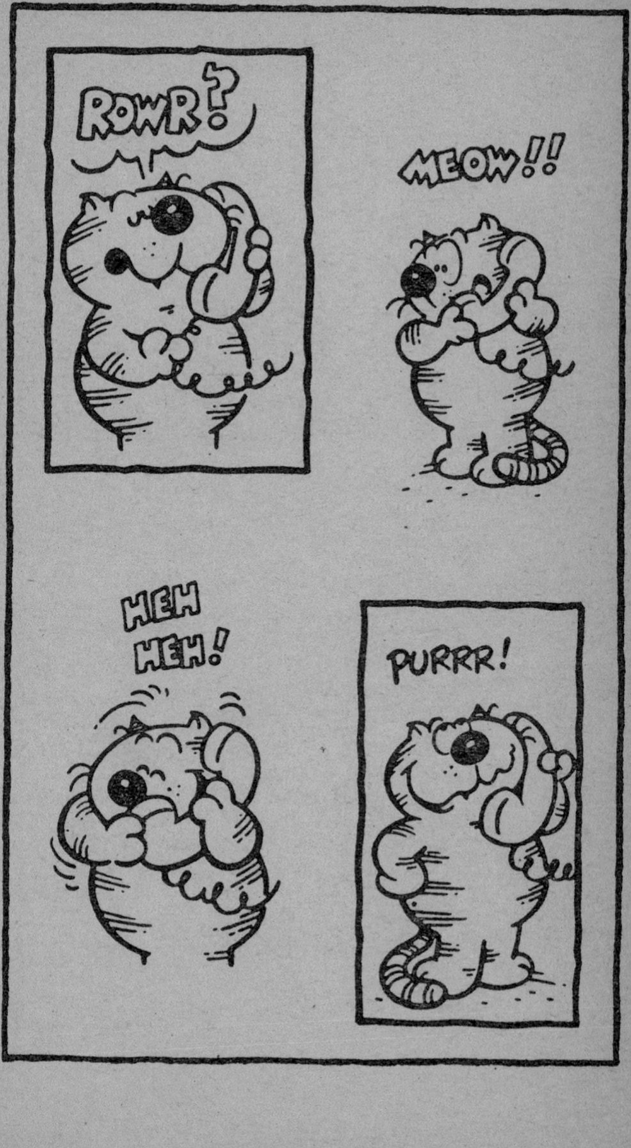
ROWR?
MEOW!!
HEH
HEH!
PURRR!

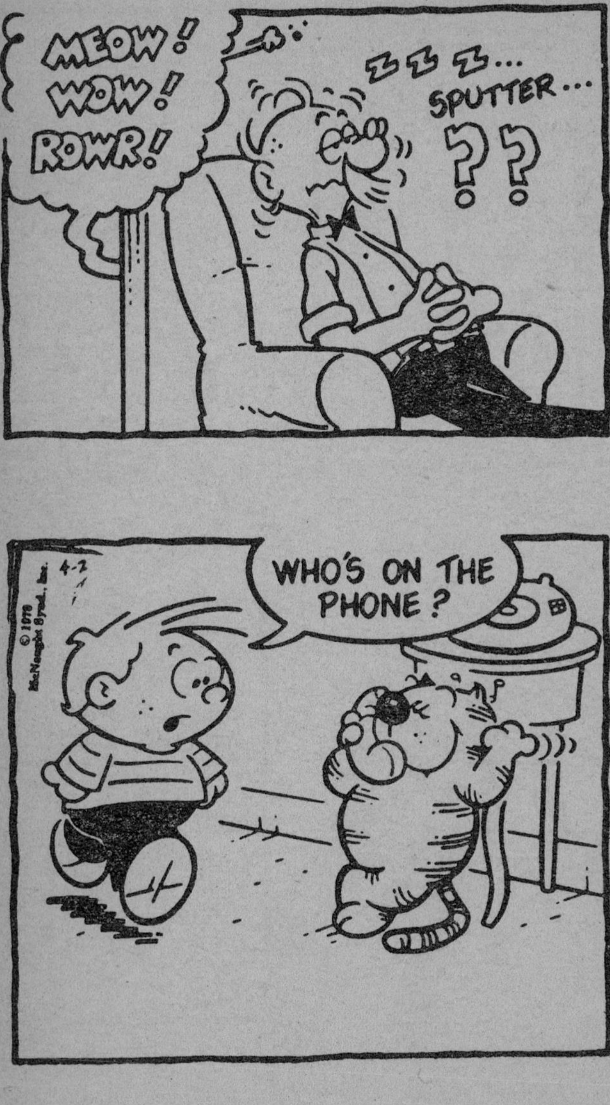
MEOW! WOW! ROWR!
Z Z Z... SPUTTER...
??
WHO'S ON THE PHONE?

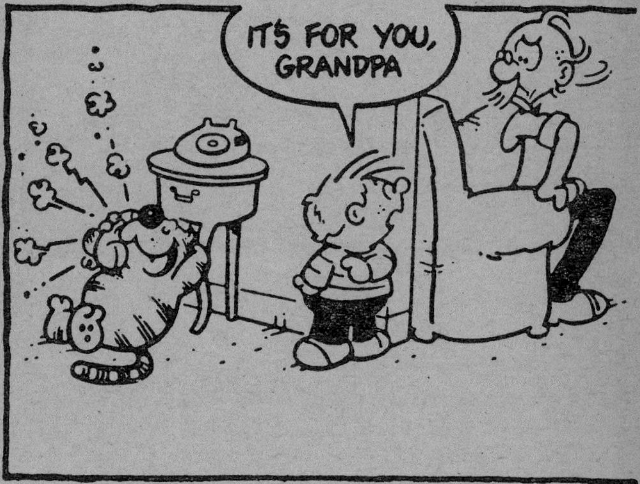
IT'S FOR YOU, GRANDPA

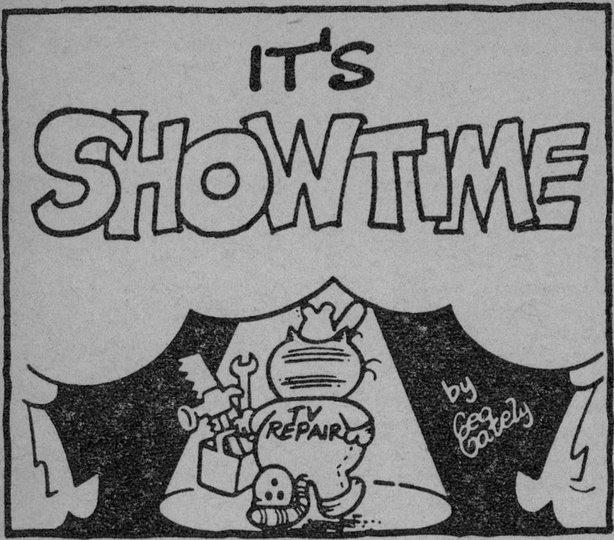
IT'S
SHOWTIME
TV REPAIR
by Geo Gately

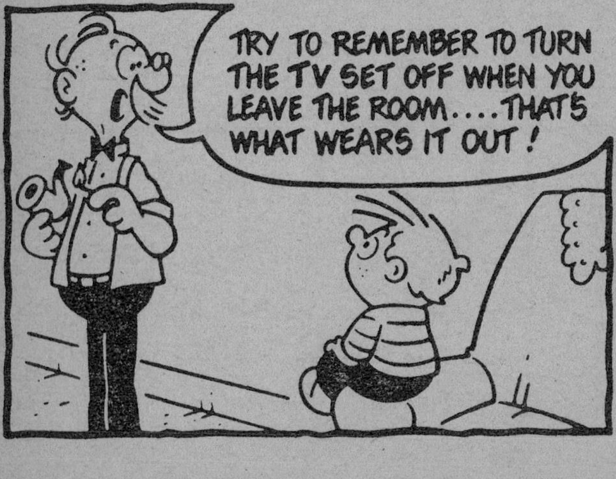
TRY TO REMEMBER TO TURN THE TV SET OFF WHEN YOU LEAVE THE ROOM....THAT'S WHAT WEARS IT OUT!

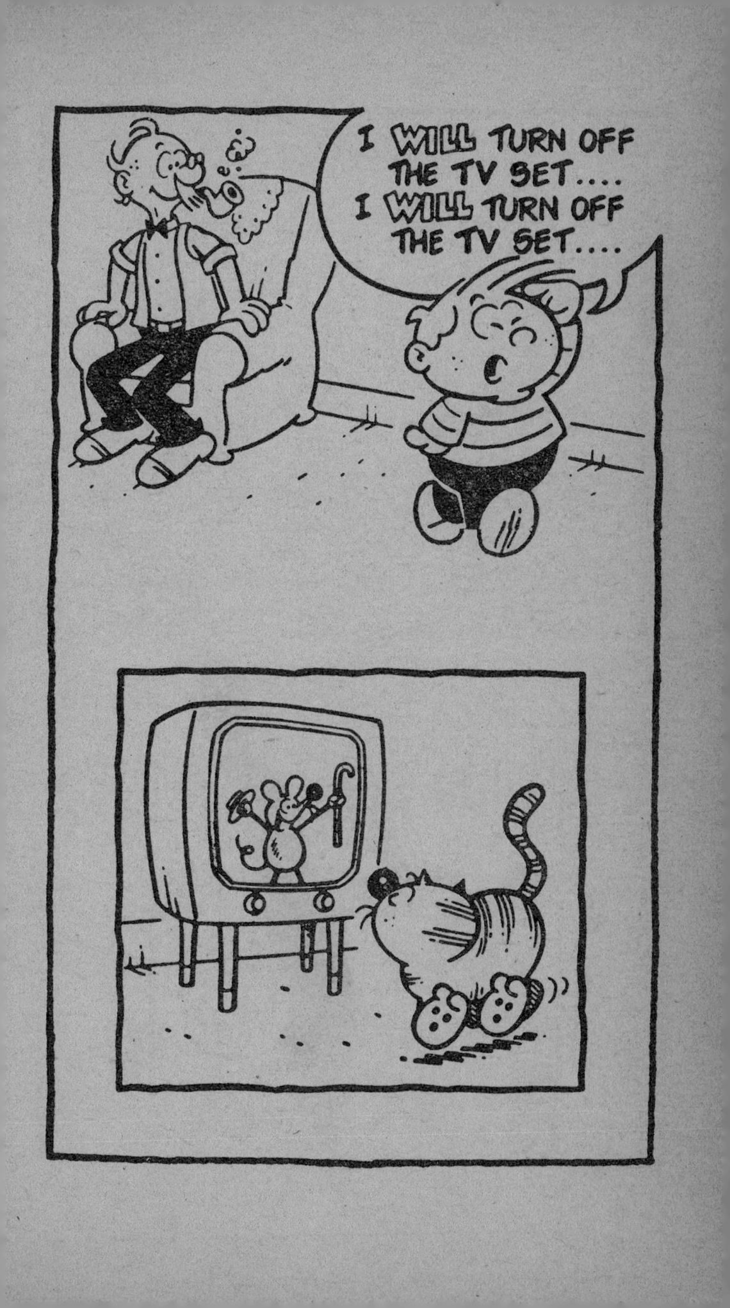
I WILL TURN OFF THE TV SET.... I WILL TURN OFF THE TV SET....

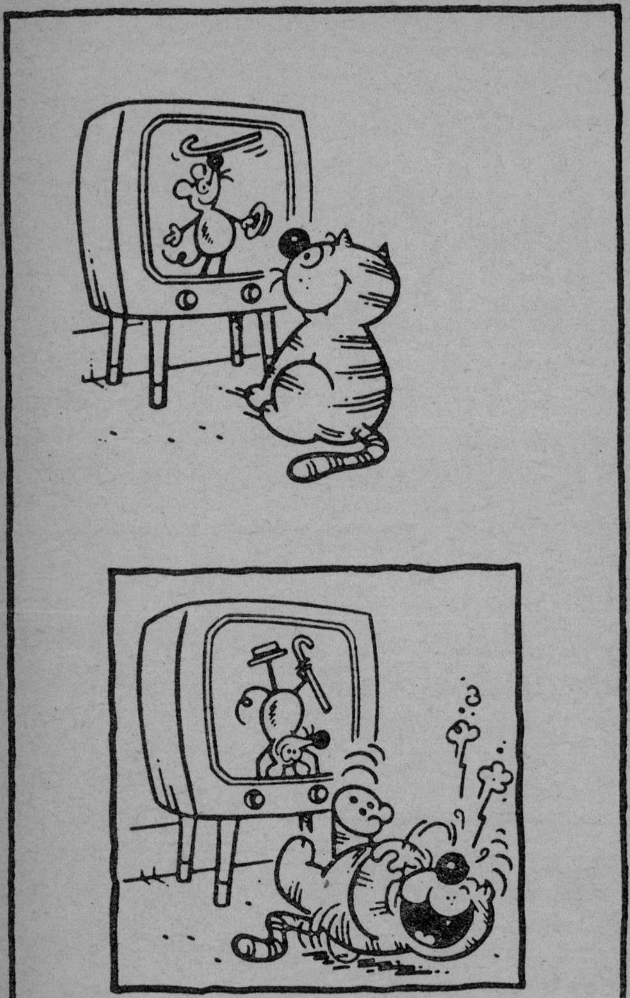

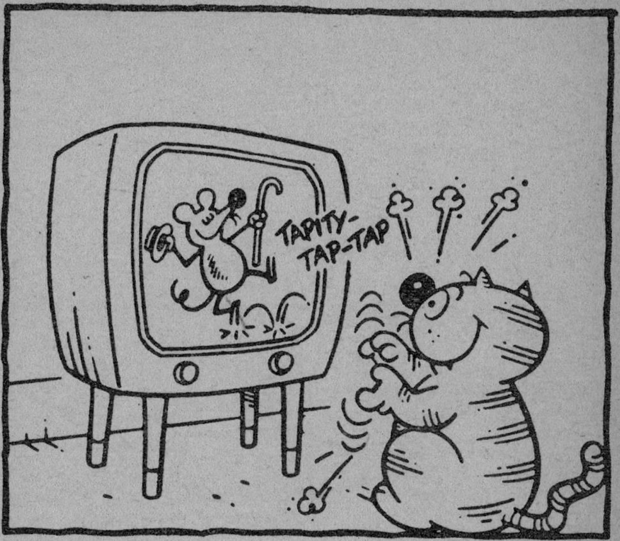
TAPITY-
TAP-TAP

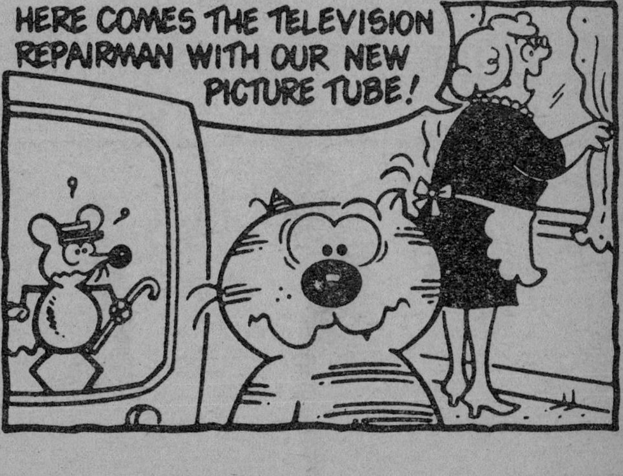
HERE COMES THE TELEVISION REPAIRMAN WITH OUR NEW PICTURE TUBE!

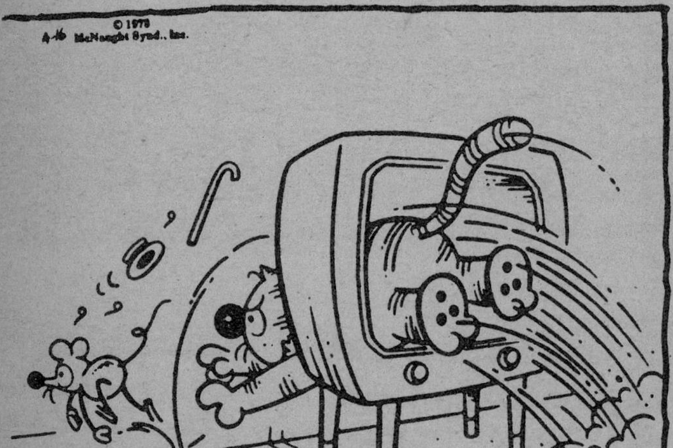
McNaught Synd., Inc.

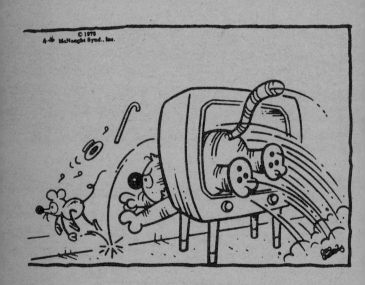

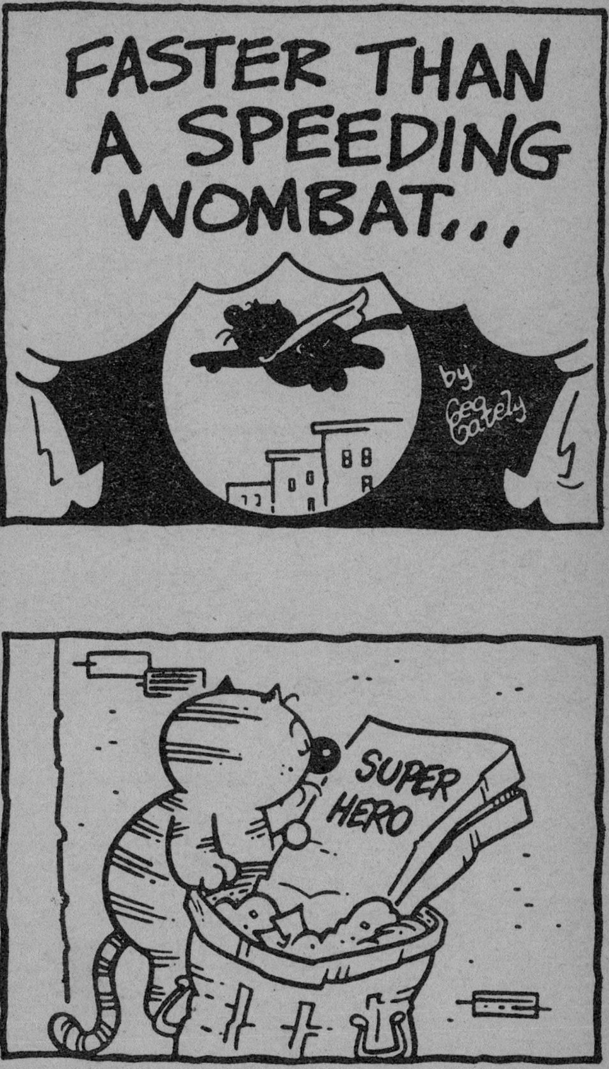
FASTER THAN A SPEEDING WOMBAT...
by Geo Gately
SUPER HERO

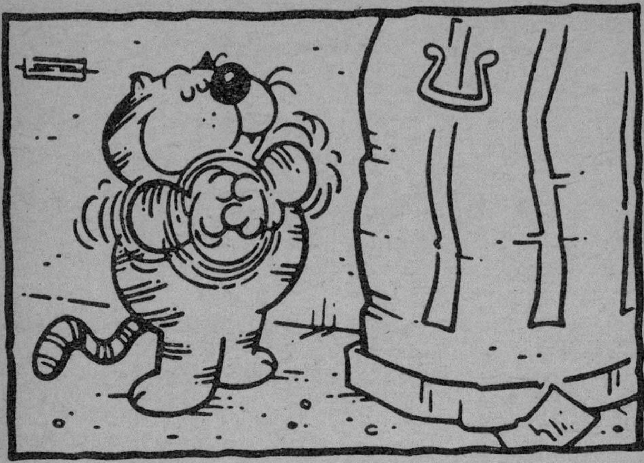

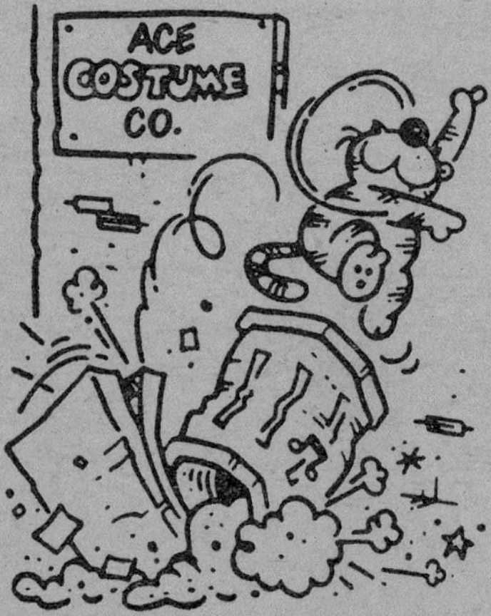
ACE
COSTUME
CO.

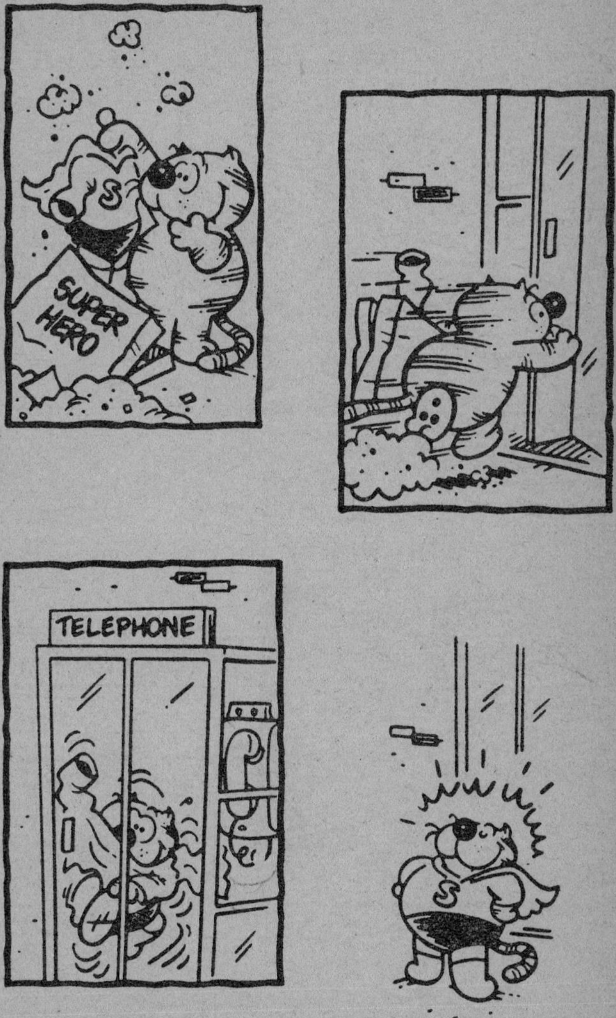
SUPER HERO
TELEPHONE

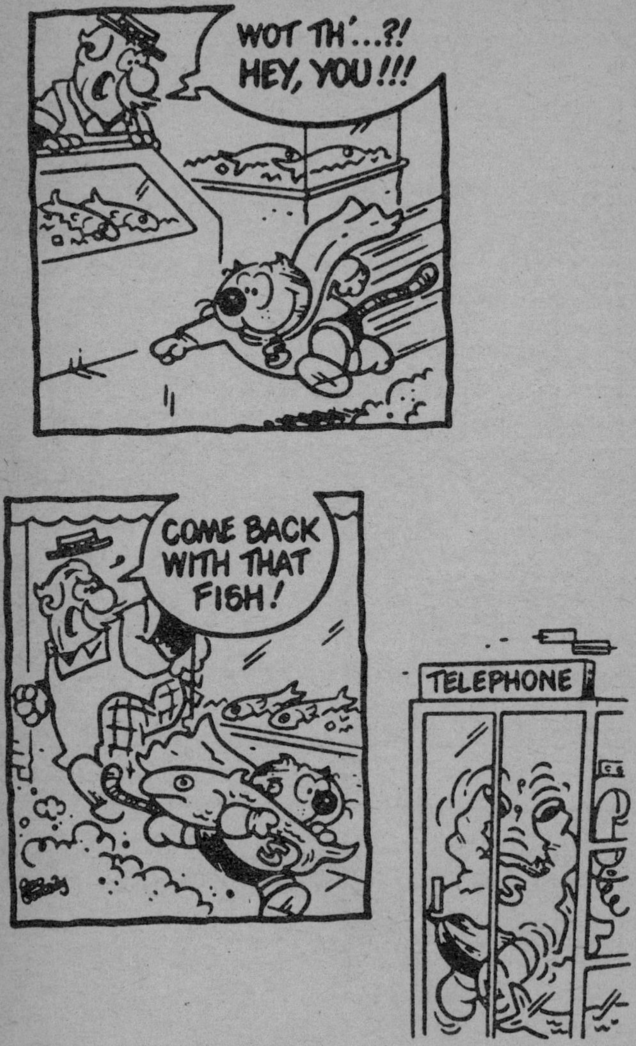
WOT TH'...?! HEY, YOU!!!
COME BACK WITH THAT FISH!
TELEPHONE

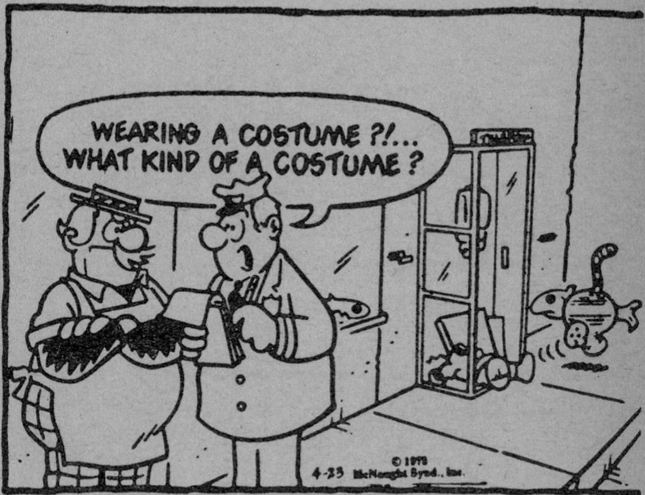
WEARING A COSTUME ?!...
WHAT KIND OF A COSTUME ?
© 1978
4-23 McNaught Synd., Inc.

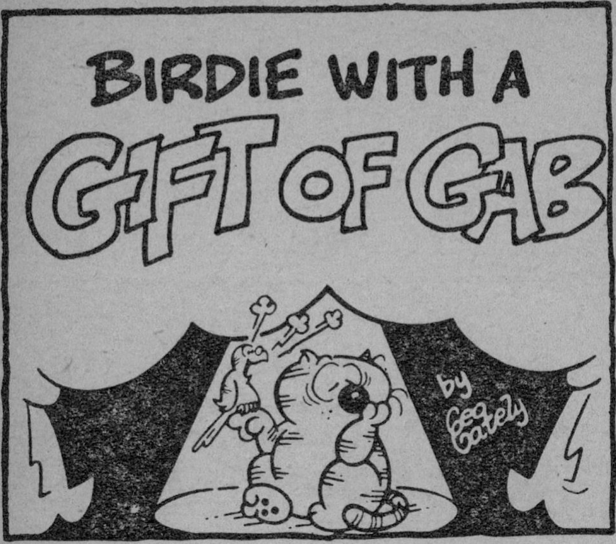
BIRDIE WITH A
GIFT OF GAB
by Geo Gately

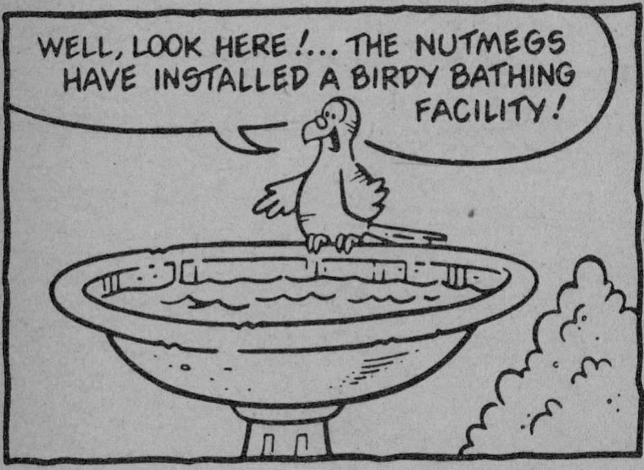
WELL, LOOK HERE!... THE NUTMEGS HAVE INSTALLED A BIRDY BATHING FACILITY!

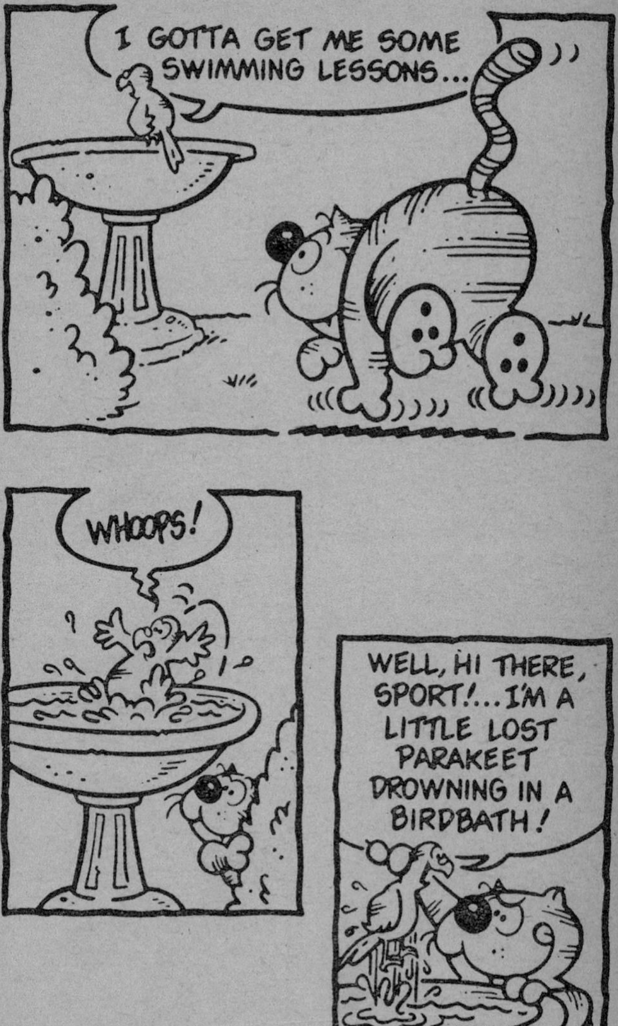
I GOTTA GET ME SOME SWIMMING LESSONS...
WHOOPS!
WELL, HI THERE, SPORT!...I'M A LITTLE LOST PARAKEET DROWNING IN A BIRDBATH!

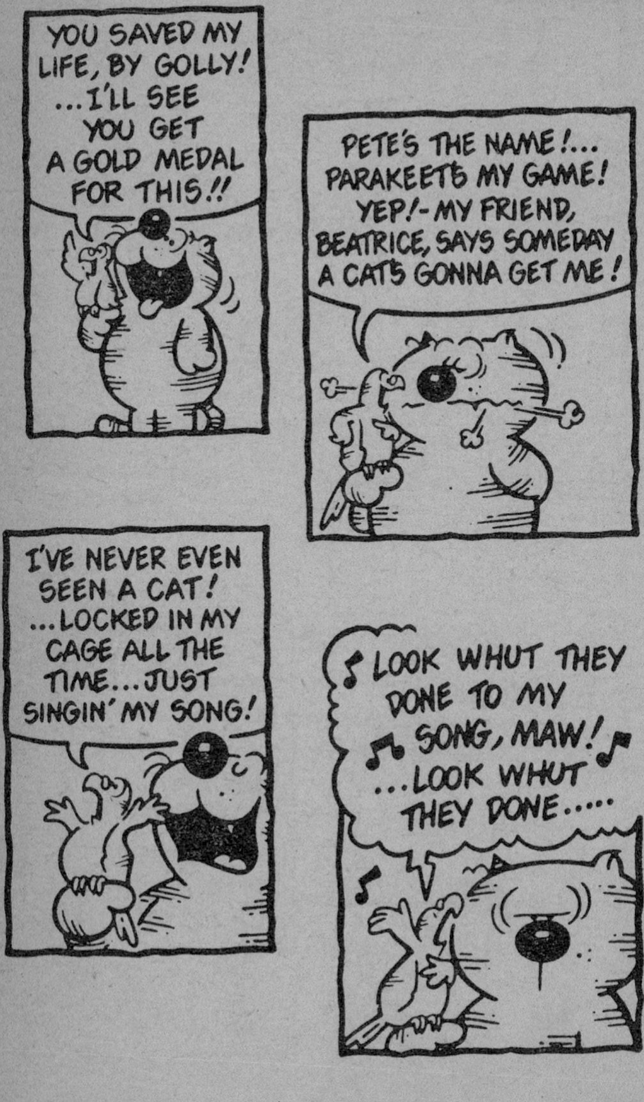
YOU SAVED MY LIFE, BY GOLLY! ...I'LL SEE YOU GET A GOLD MEDAL FOR THIS!!
PETE'S THE NAME!... PARAKEET'S MY GAME! YEP!- MY FRIEND, BEATRICE, SAYS SOMEDAY A CAT'S GONNA GET ME!
I'VE NEVER EVEN SEEN A CAT! ...LOCKED IN MY CAGE ALL THE TIME... JUST SINGIN' MY SONG!
LOOK WHUT THEY DONE TO MY SONG, MAW! ...LOOK WHUT THEY DONE.....

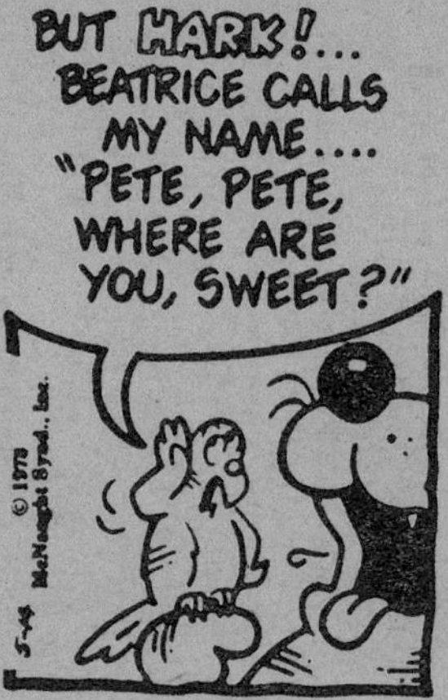
BUT HARK!... BEATRICE CALLS MY NAME.... "PETE, PETE, WHERE ARE YOU, SWEET?"
© 1978 McNaught Synd., Inc.
5-4

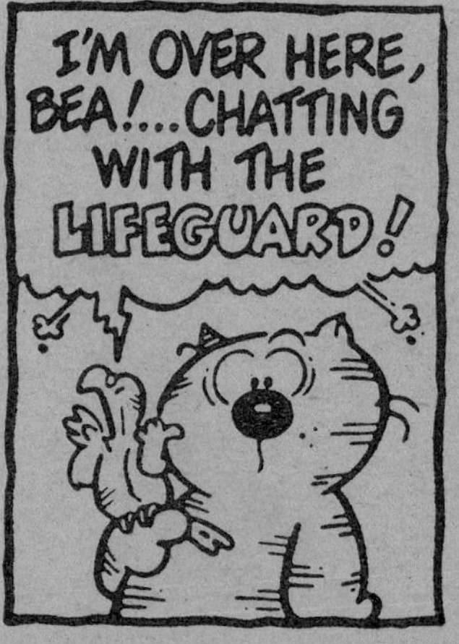
I'M OVER HERE, BEA!...CHATTING WITH THE LIFEGUARD!

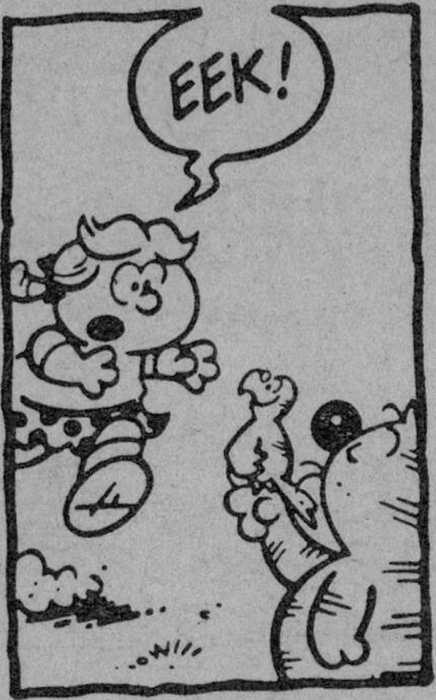
EEK!

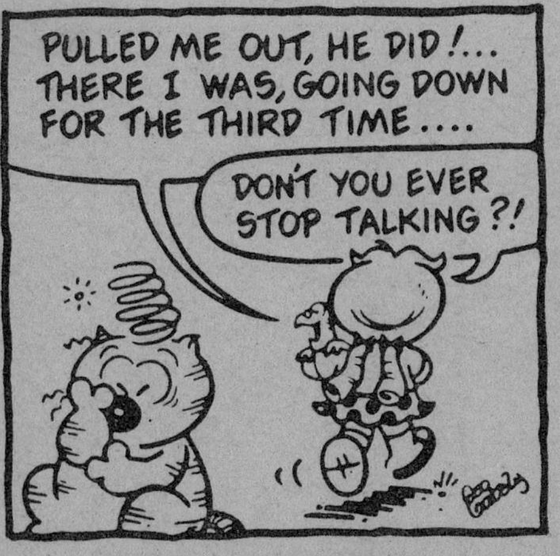
PULLED ME OUT, HE DID!... THERE I WAS, GOING DOWN FOR THE THIRD TIME....
DON'T YOU EVER STOP TALKING?!

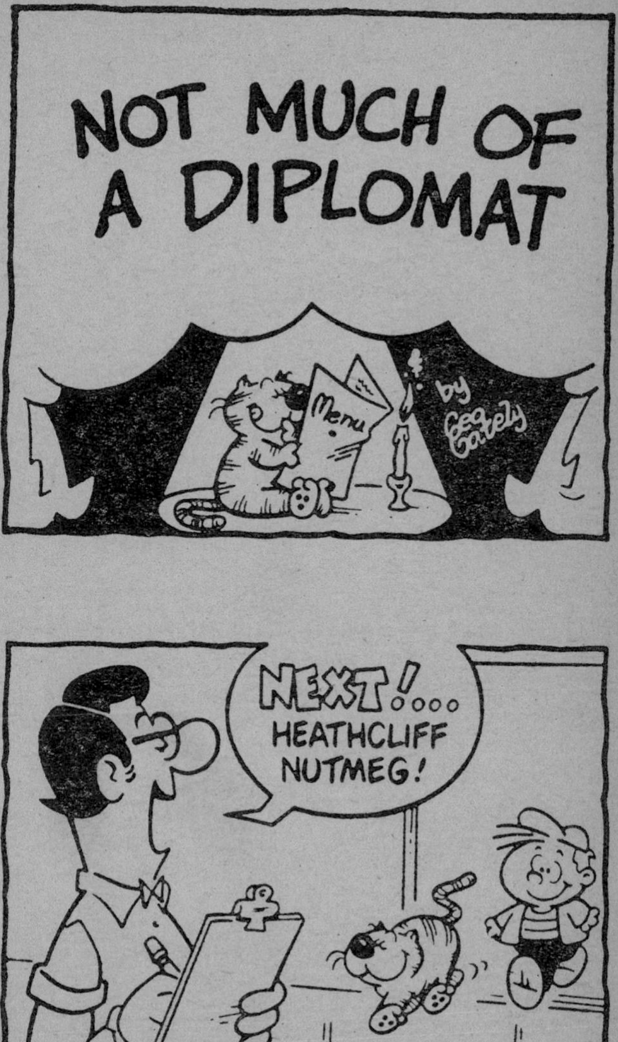
NOT MUCH OF A DIPLOMAT
Menu
by Geo Gately
NEXT!...
HEATHCLIFF NUTMEG!

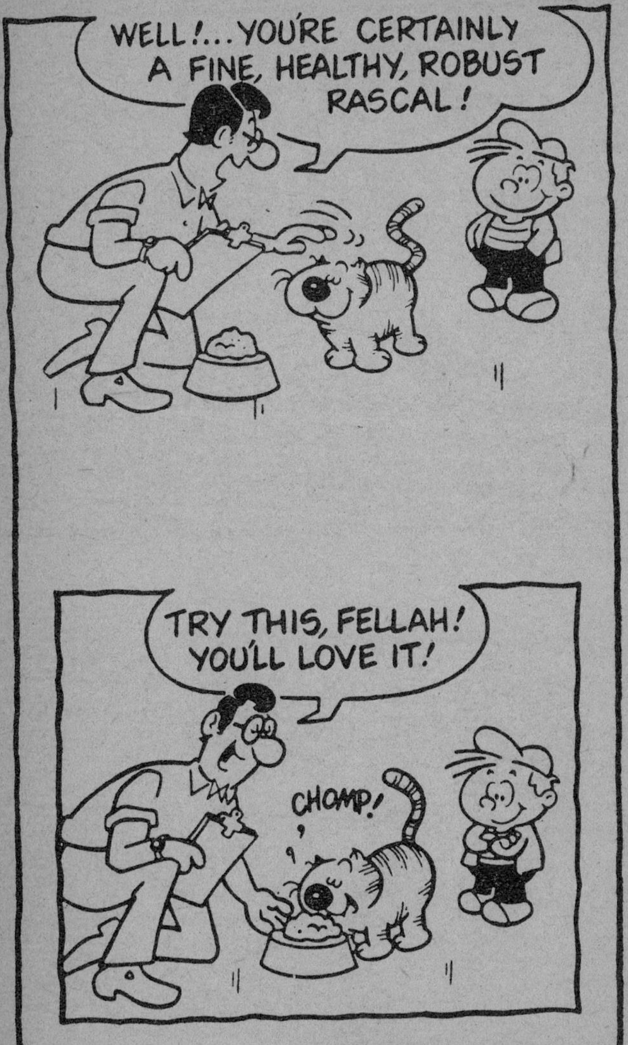
WELL!...YOU'RE CERTAINLY A FINE, HEALTHY, ROBUST RASCAL!
TRY THIS, FELLAH! YOU'LL LOVE IT!
CHOMP!

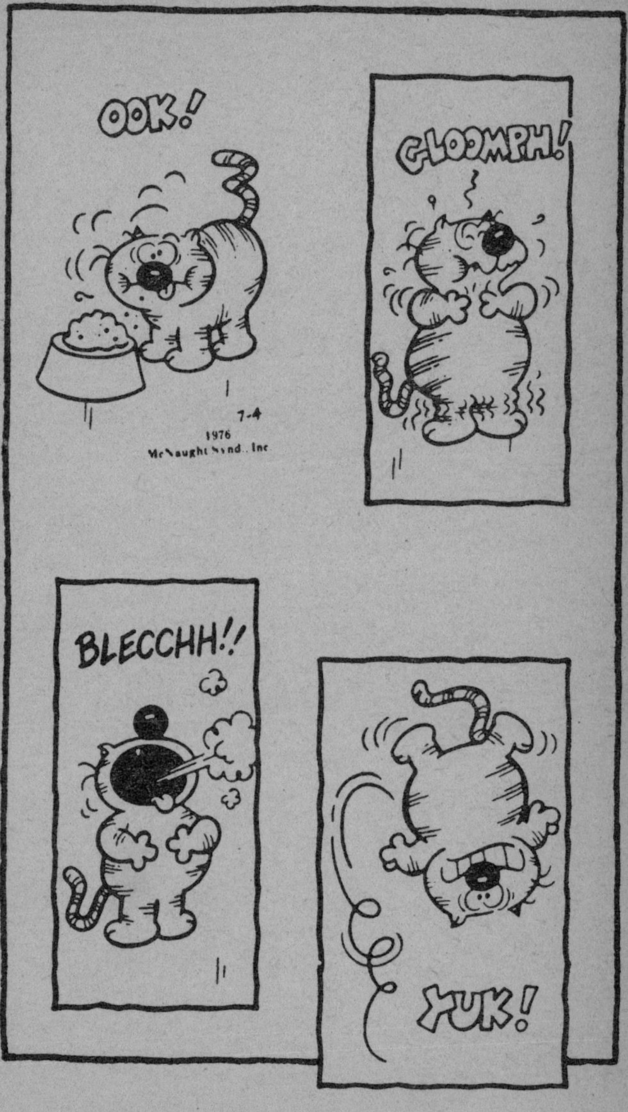
OOK!
7-4
1976
McNaught Synd., Inc.
GLOOMPH!
BLECCHH!!
YUK!

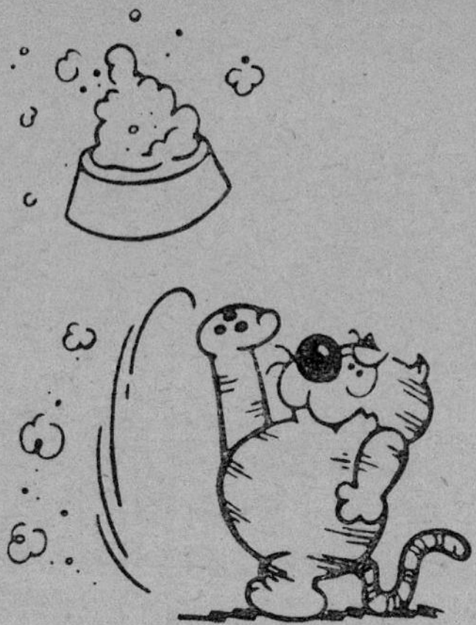

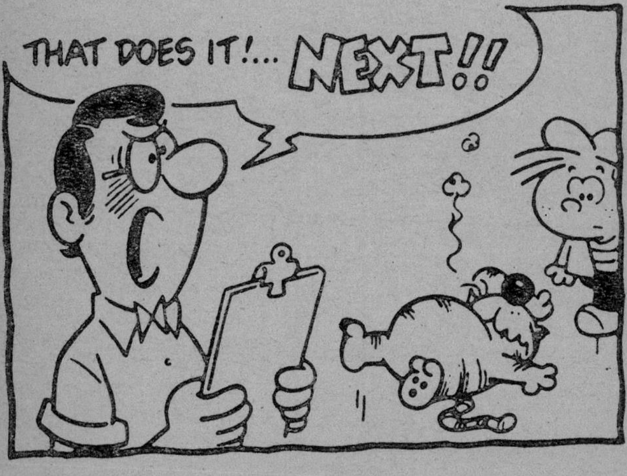
THAT DOES IT!... NEXT!!

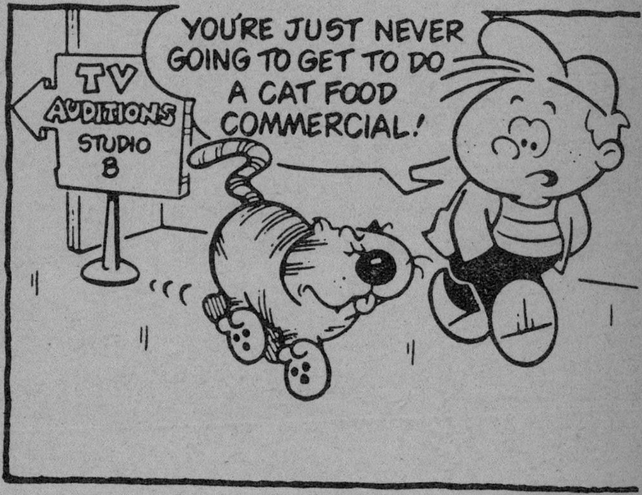
TV AUDITIONS STUDIO 8
YOU'RE JUST NEVER GOING TO GET TO DO A CAT FOOD COMMERCIAL!

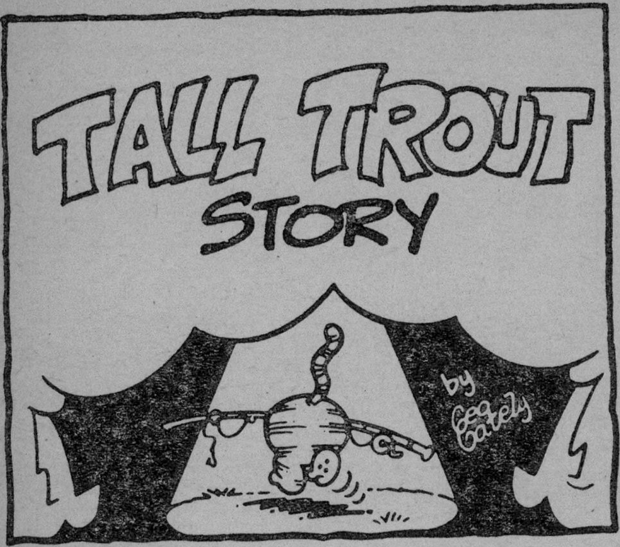
TALL TROUT
STORY
by

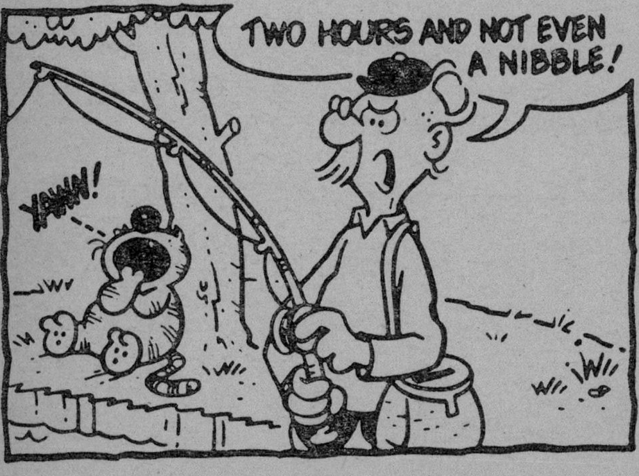
TWO HOURS AND NOT EVEN A NIBBLE!
YAWN!

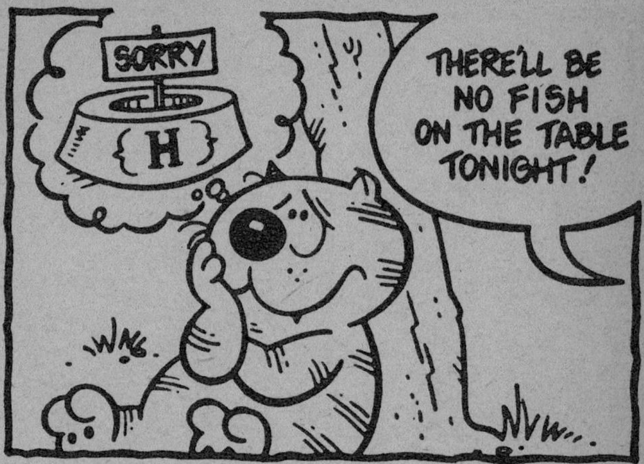
SORRY
H
THERE'LL BE NO FISH ON THE TABLE TONIGHT!

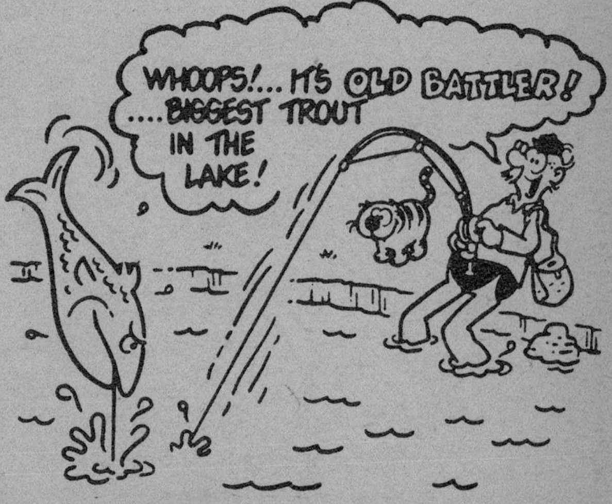
WHOOPS!... IT'S OLD BATTLER! ....BIGGEST TROUT IN THE LAKE!

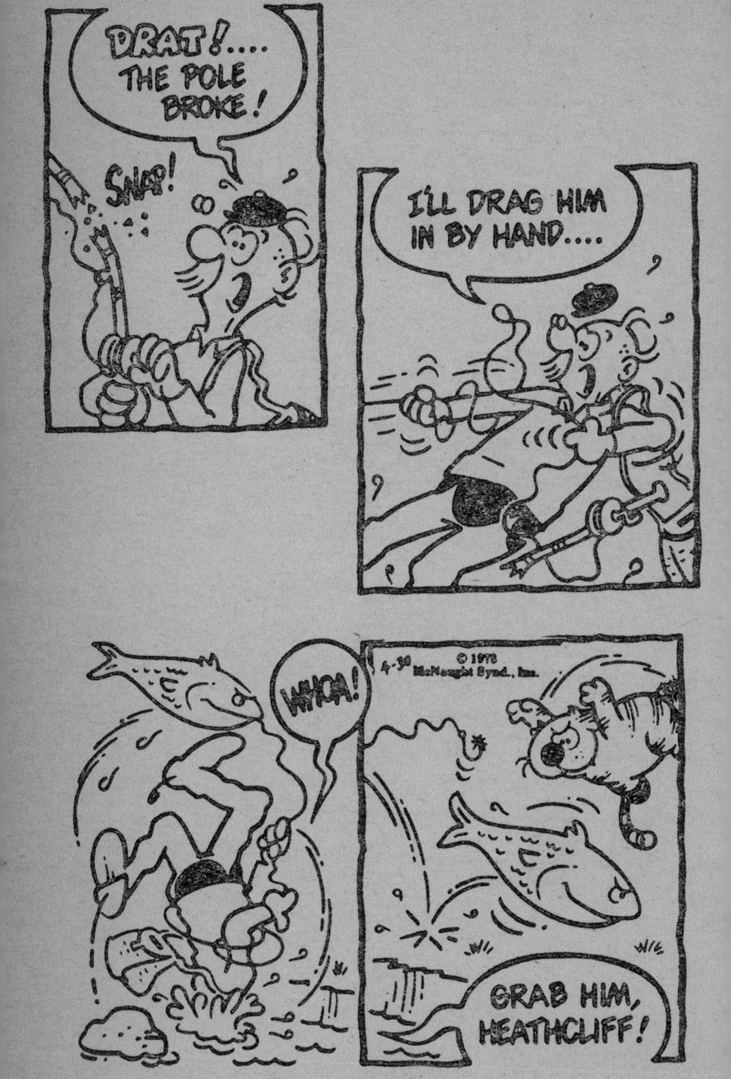
DRAT!.... THE POLE BROKE!
SNAP!
I'LL DRAG HIM IN BY HAND....
WHOA!
4-30 © 1978 McNaught Synd., Inc.
GRAB HIM, HEATHCLIFF!

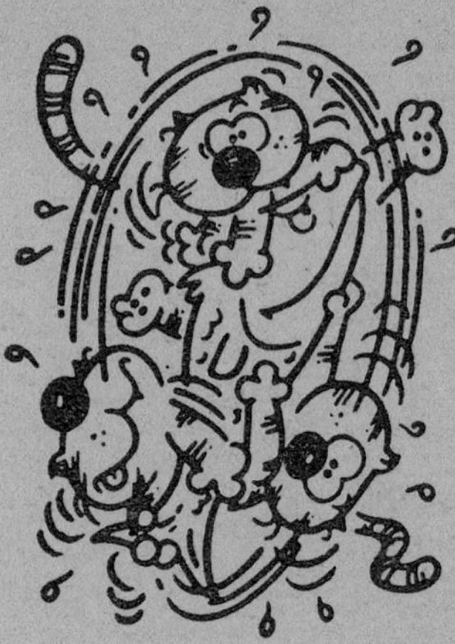

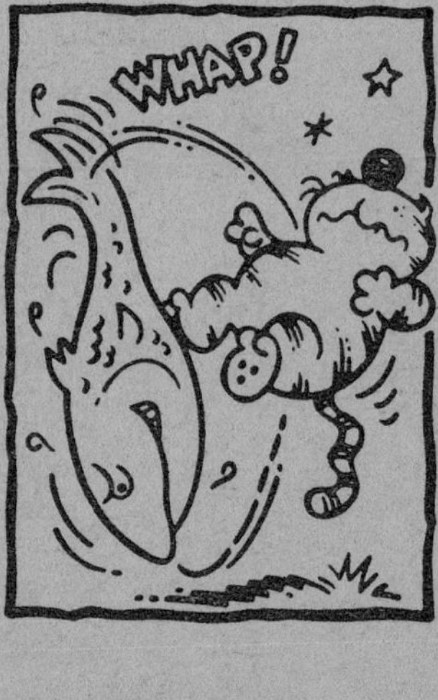
WHAP!

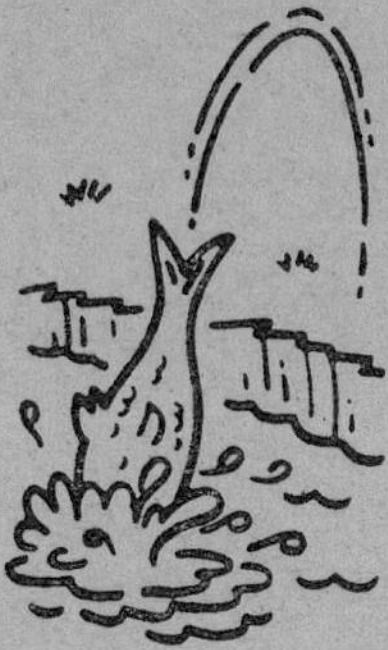

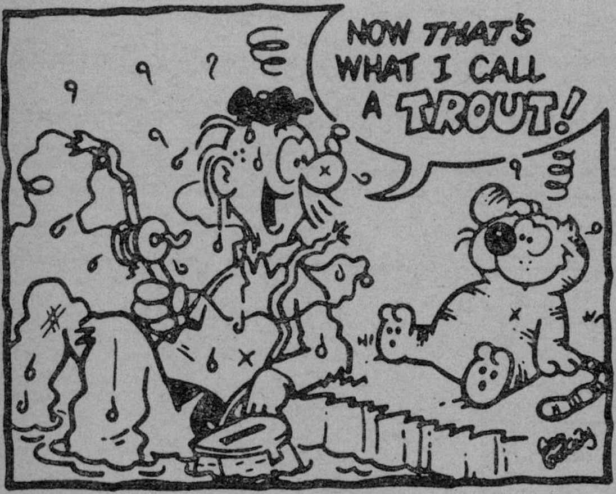
NOW THAT'S WHAT I CALL A TROUT!

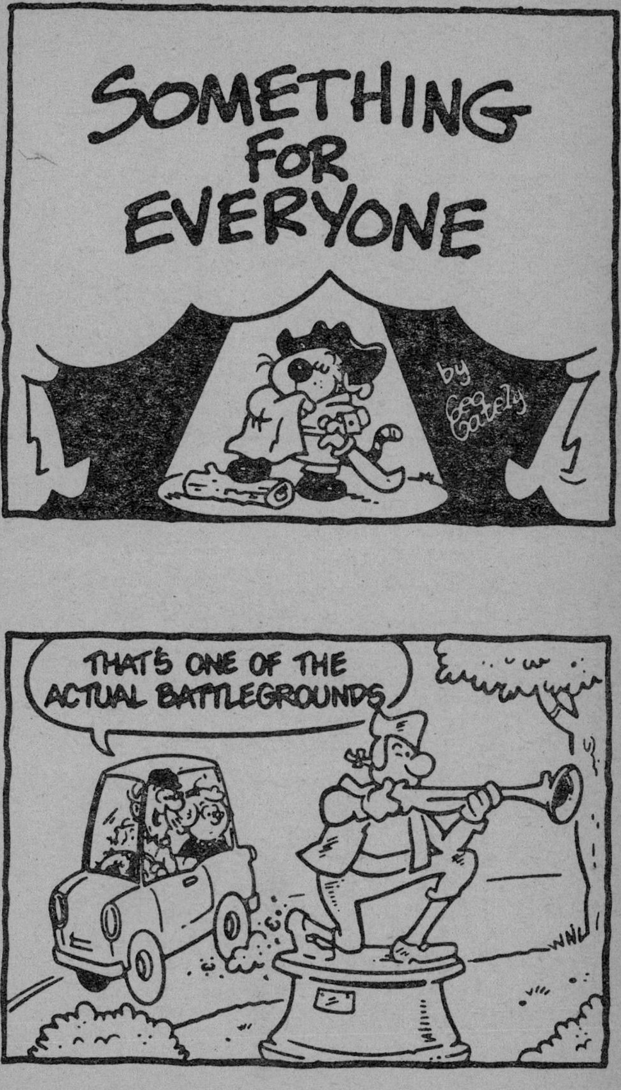
SOMETHING FOR EVERYONE
by Geo Gately
THAT'S ONE OF THE ACTUAL BATTLEGROUNDS

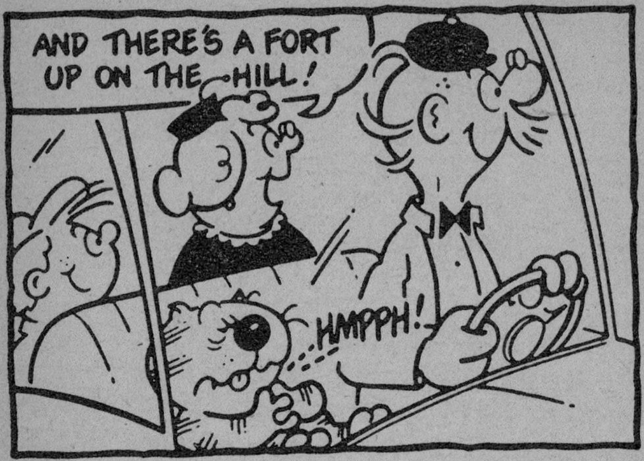
AND THERE'S A FORT UP ON THE HILL!
HMPPH!

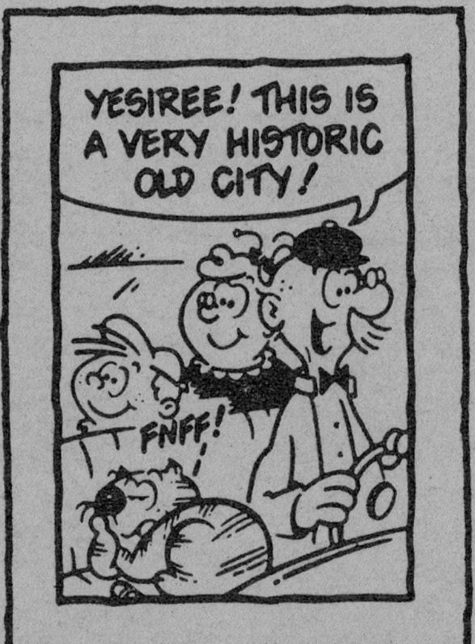
YESIREE! THIS IS A VERY HISTORIC OLD CITY!
FNFF!

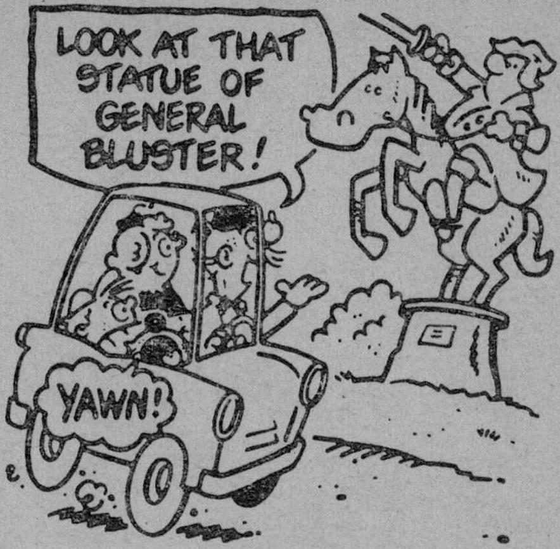
LOOK AT THAT STATUE OF GENERAL BLUSTER!
YAWN!

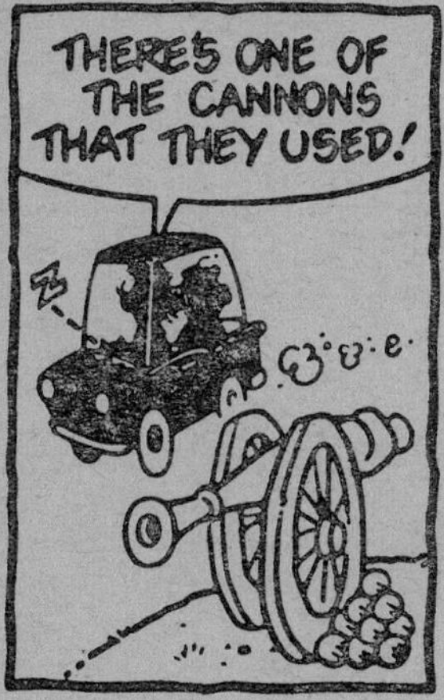
THERE'S ONE OF THE CANNONS THAT THEY USED!

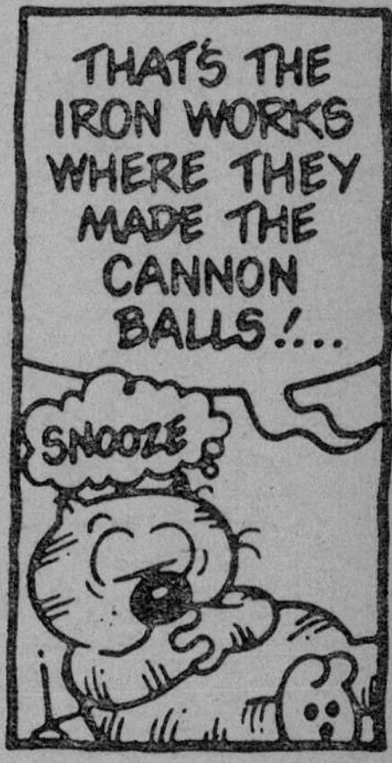
THAT'S THE IRON WORKS WHERE THEY MADE THE CANNON BALLS!...
SNOOZE

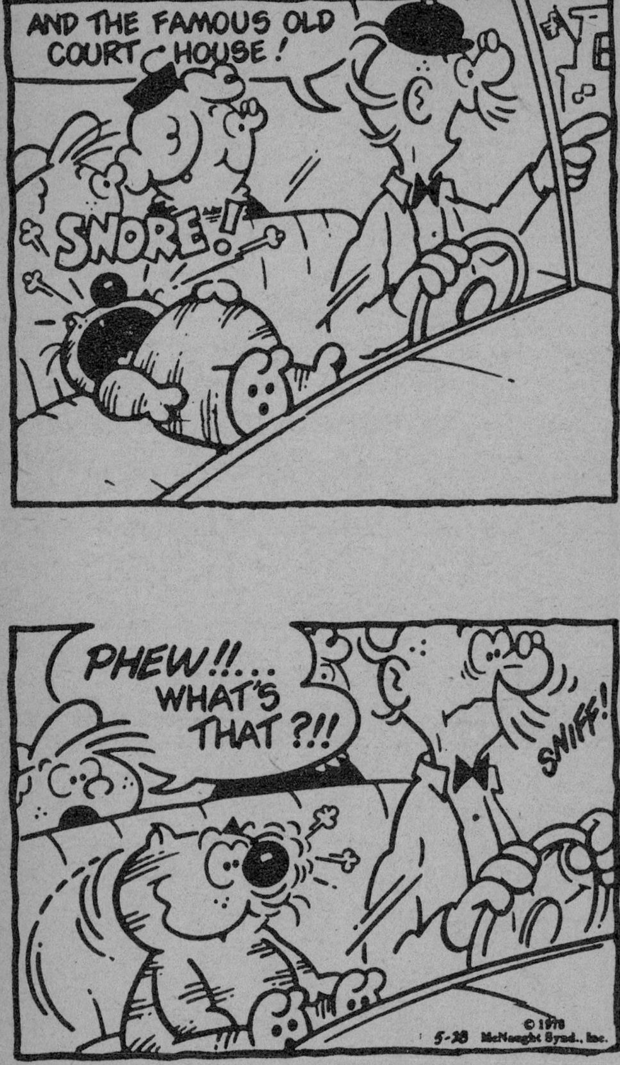
AND THE FAMOUS OLD COURT HOUSE!
SNORE!
PHEW!!... WHAT'S THAT?!!
SNIFF!
© 1978
5-28 McNaught Synd., Inc.

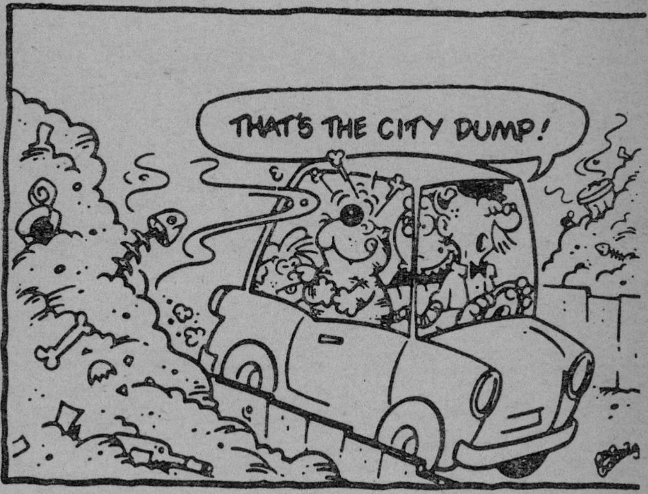
THAT'S THE CITY DUMP!

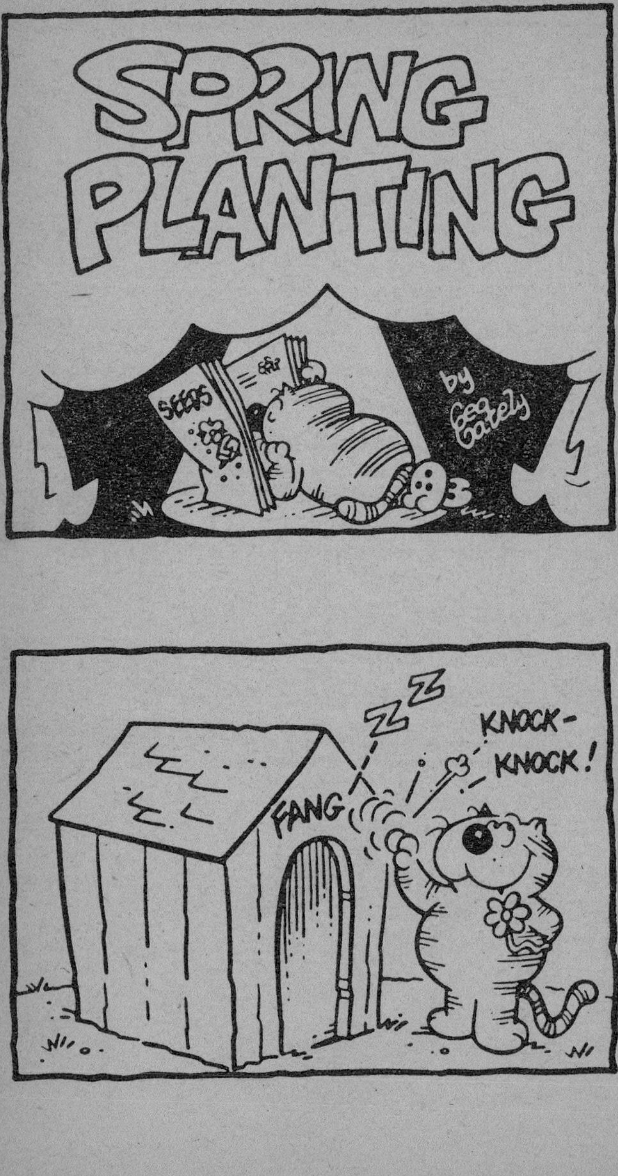
SPRING PLANTING
SEEDS
by Geo Gately
FANG
Z Z
KNOCK-KNOCK!

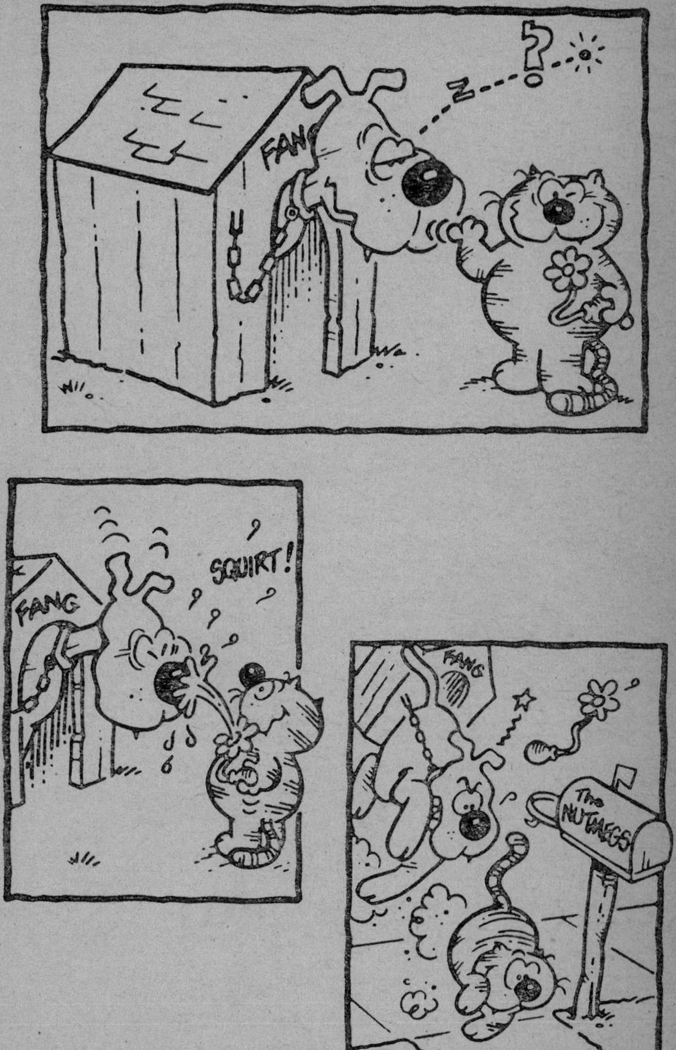
FANG
Z
?
FANG
SQUIRT!
FANG
The NUTMEGS

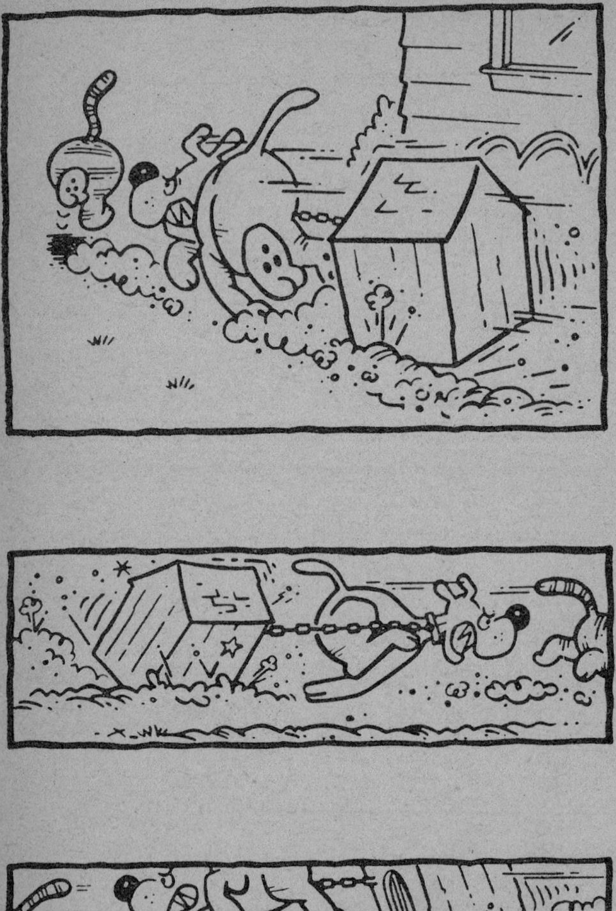

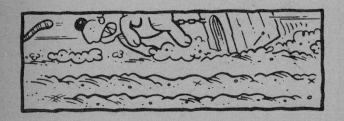

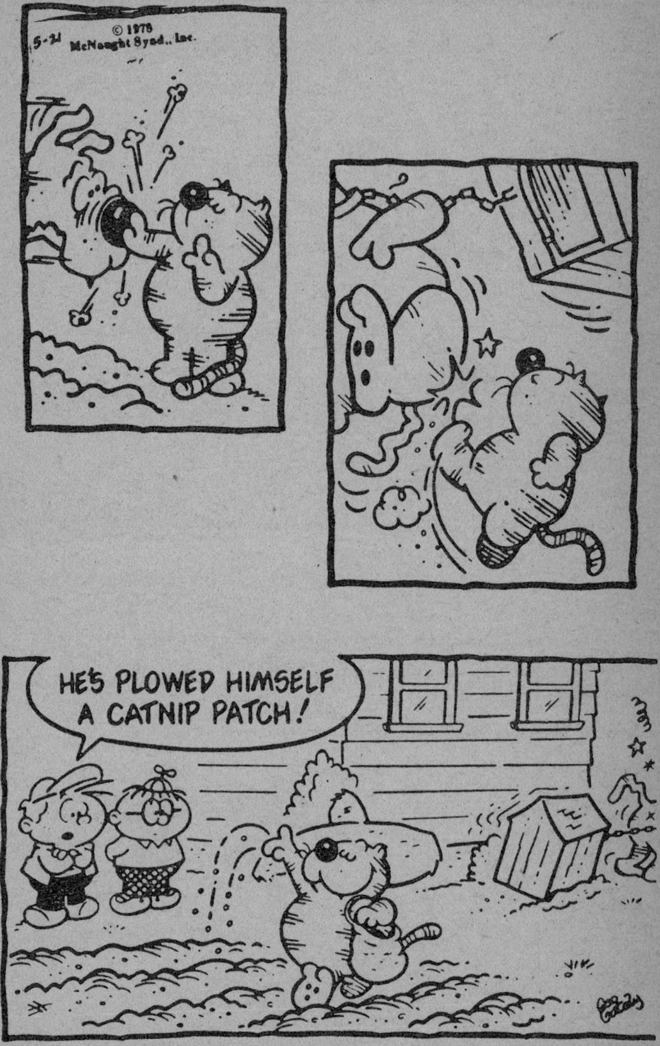
5-21
© 1978
McNaught Synd., Inc.
HE'S PLOWED HIMSELF A CATNIP PATCH!

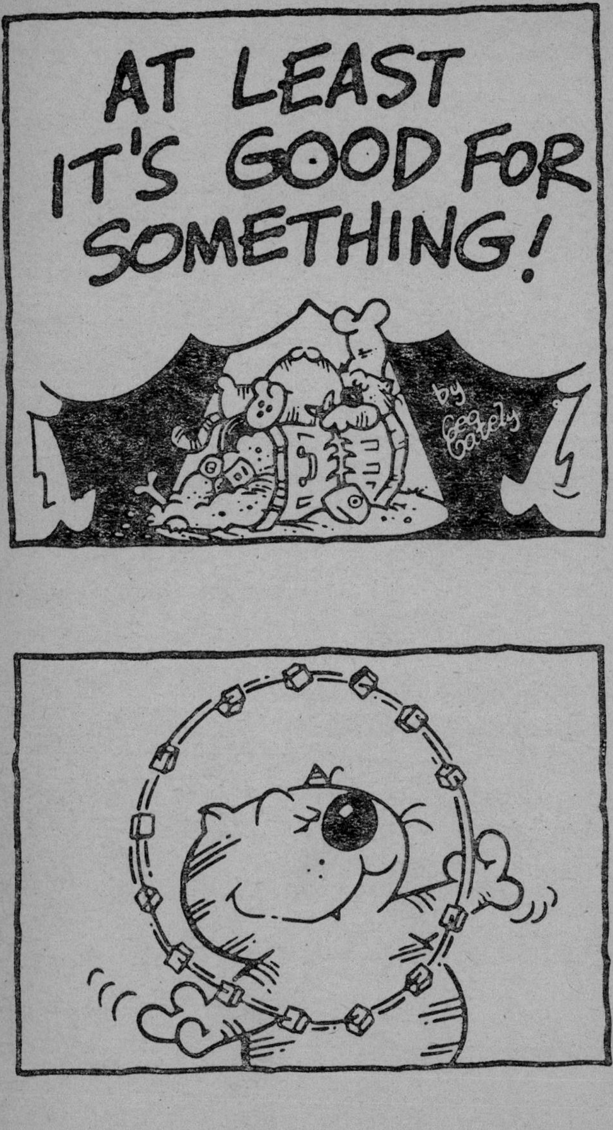
AT LEAST IT'S GOOD FOR SOMETHING!

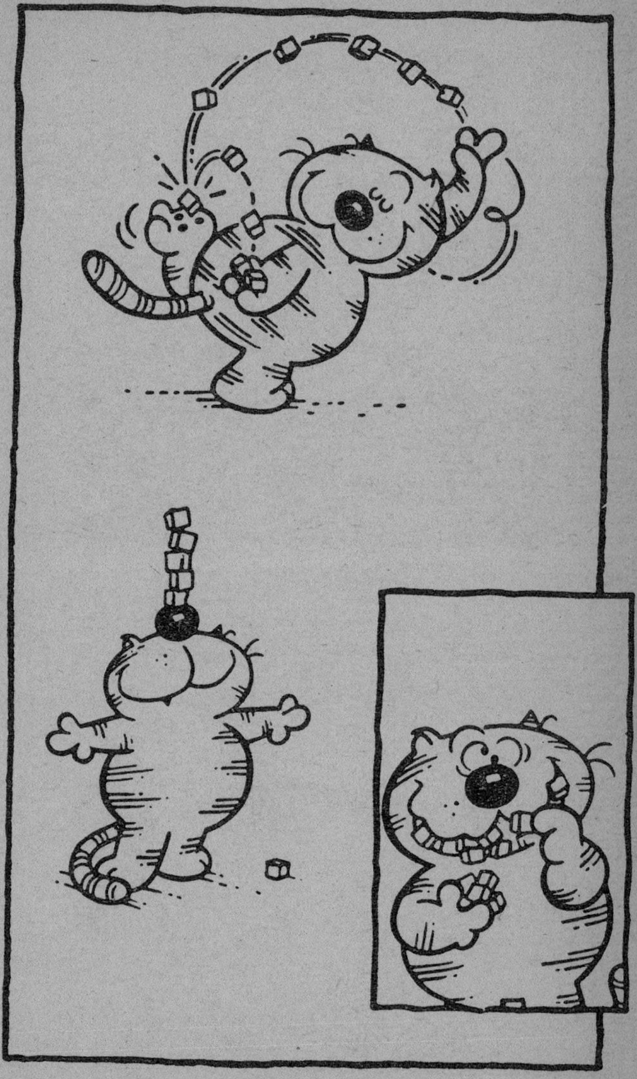

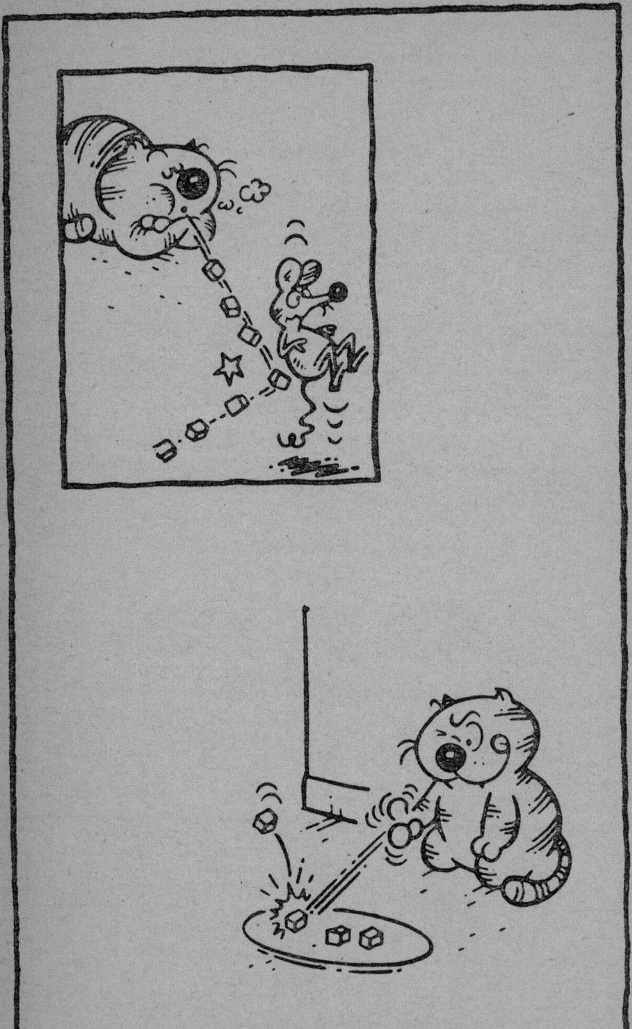

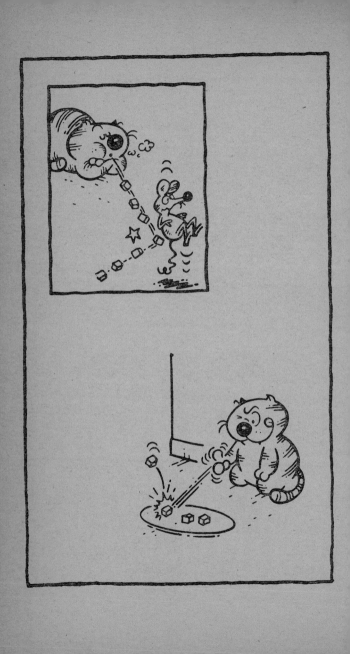

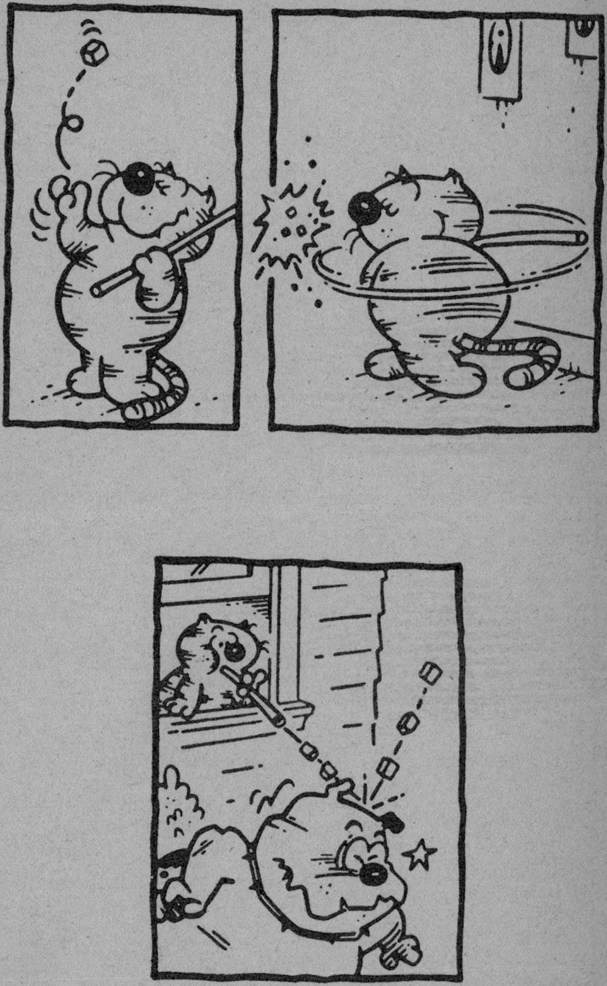

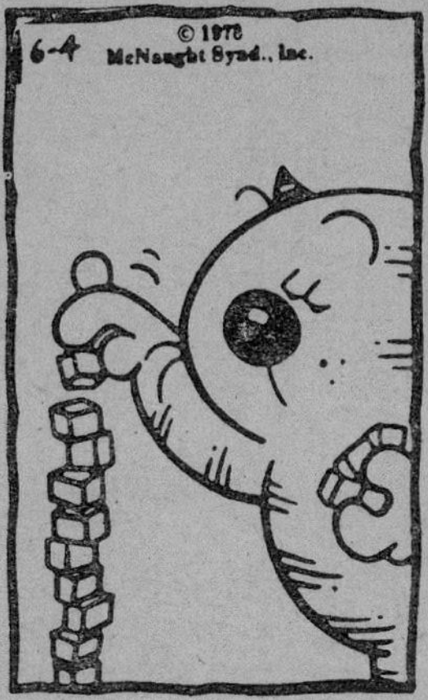
6-4
© 1978
McNaught Synd., Inc.

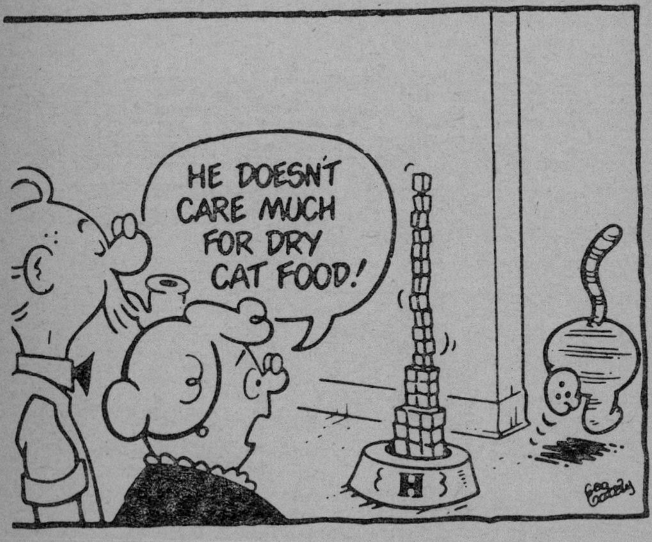
HE DOESN'T CARE MUCH FOR DRY CAT FOOD!
H

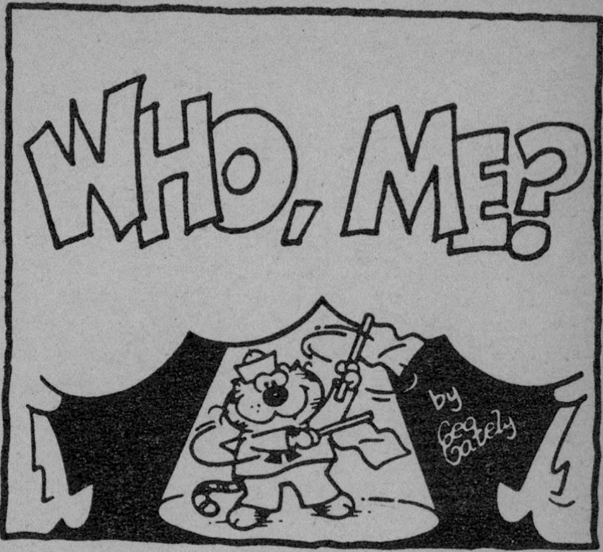
WHO, ME?
by
Geo Gately

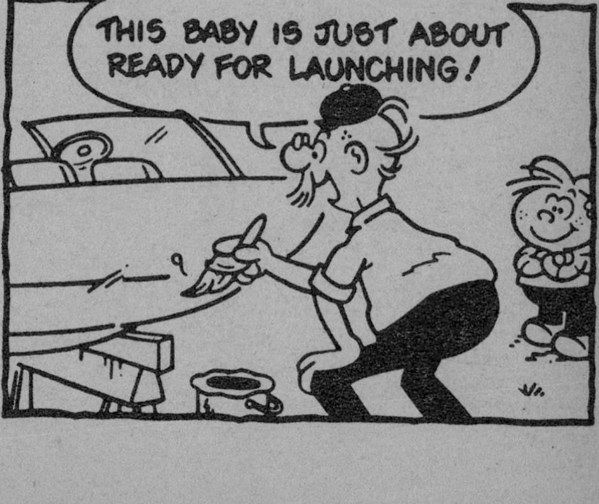
THIS BABY IS JUST ABOUT READY FOR LAUNCHING!

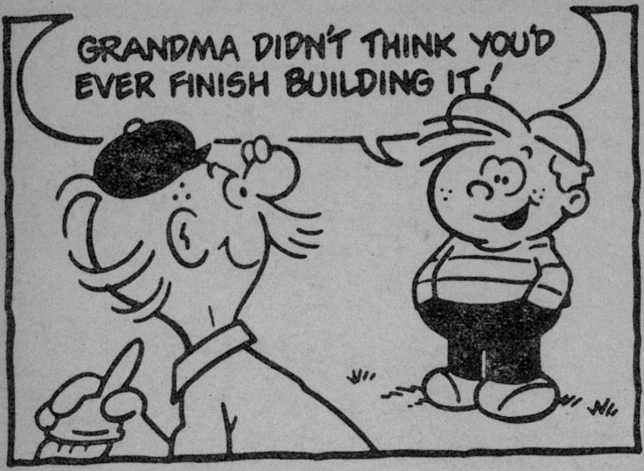
GRANDMA DIDN'T THINK YOU'D EVER FINISH BUILDING IT!

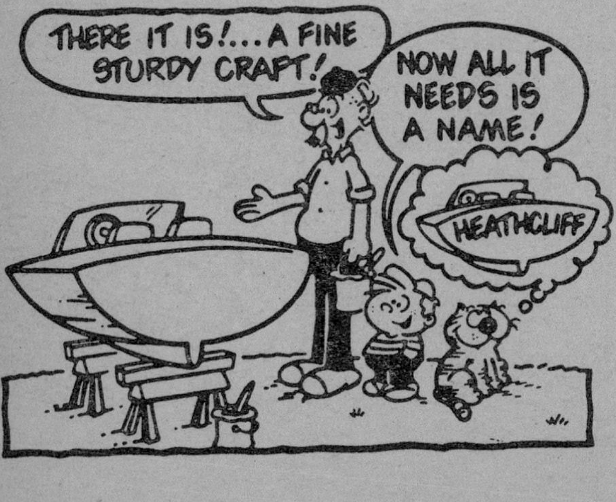
THERE IT IS!... A FINE STURDY CRAFT!
NOW ALL IT NEEDS IS A NAME!
HEATHCLIFF

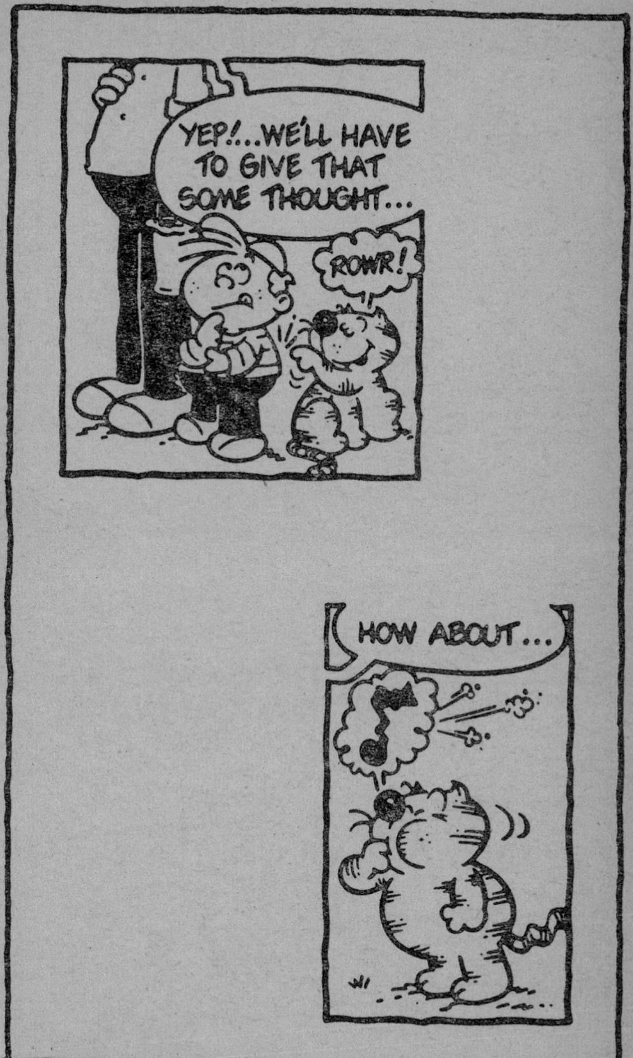
YEP!...WE'LL HAVE TO GIVE THAT SOME THOUGHT...
ROWR!
HOW ABOUT...

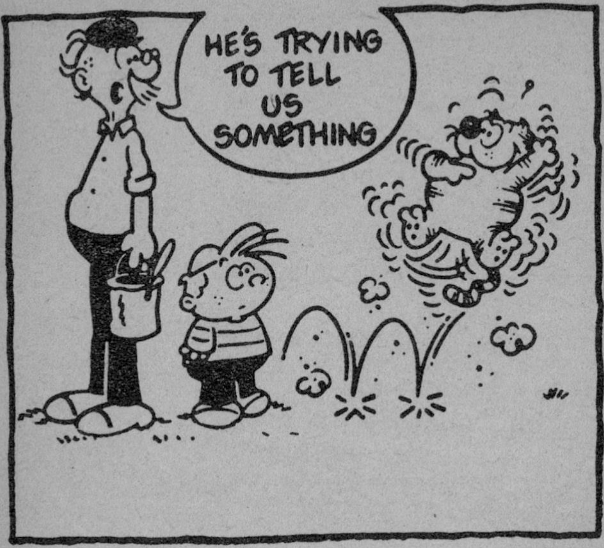
HE'S TRYING TO TELL US SOMETHING

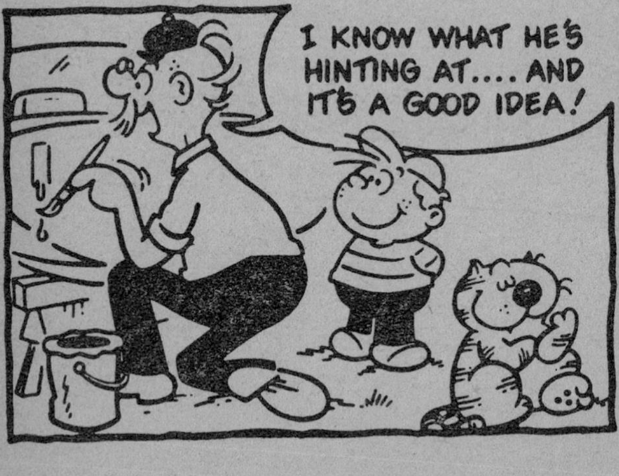
I KNOW WHAT HE'S HINTING AT.... AND IT'S A GOOD IDEA!

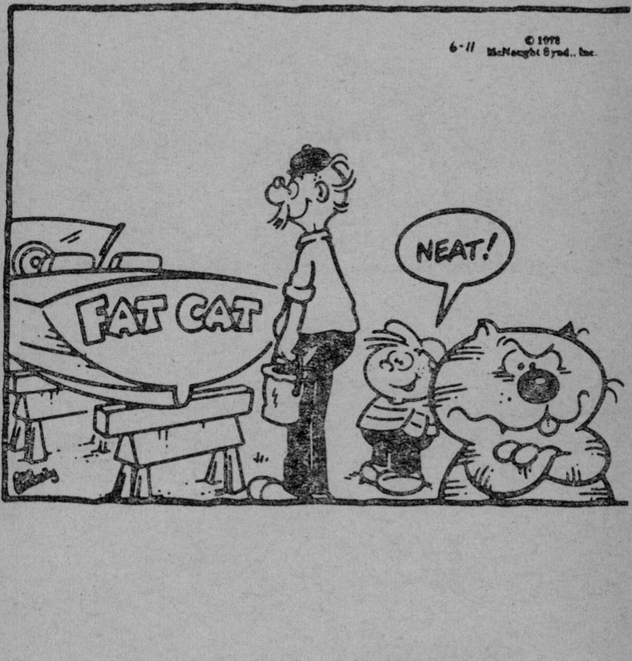

6-11
© 1978 McNaught Synd., Inc.
FAT CAT
NEAT!

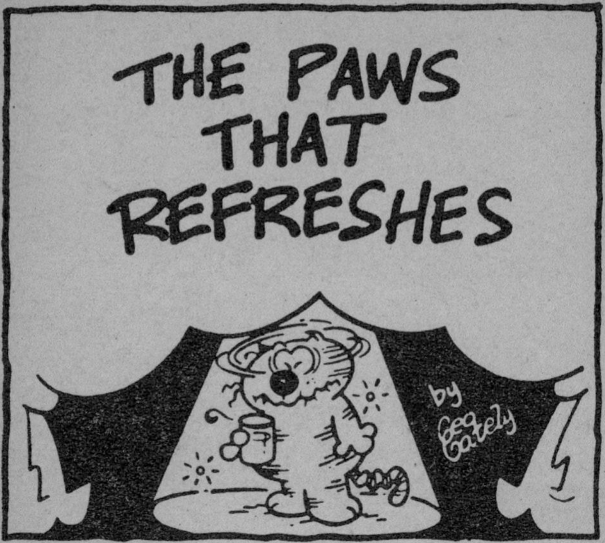
THE PAWS
THAT
REFRESHES
by Geo Gately

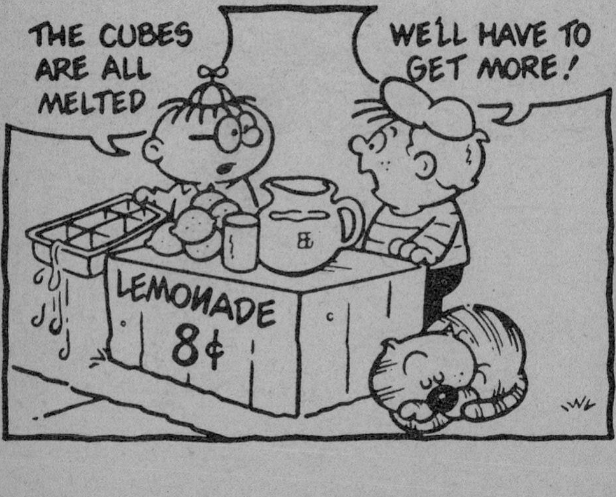
THE CUBES ARE ALL MELTED
WE'LL HAVE TO GET MORE!
LEMONADE
8¢

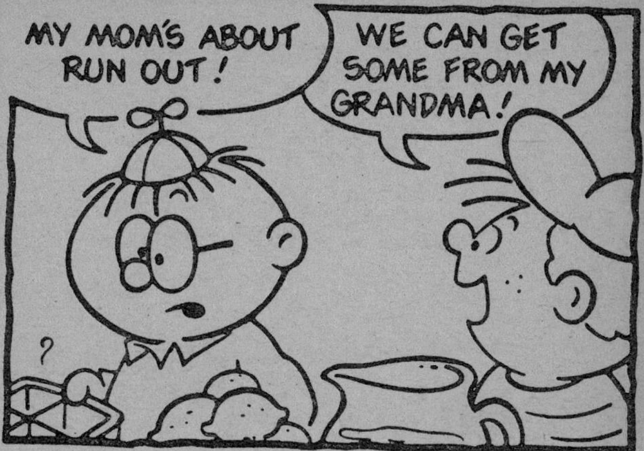
MY MOM'S ABOUT RUN OUT!
WE CAN GET SOME FROM MY GRANDMA!

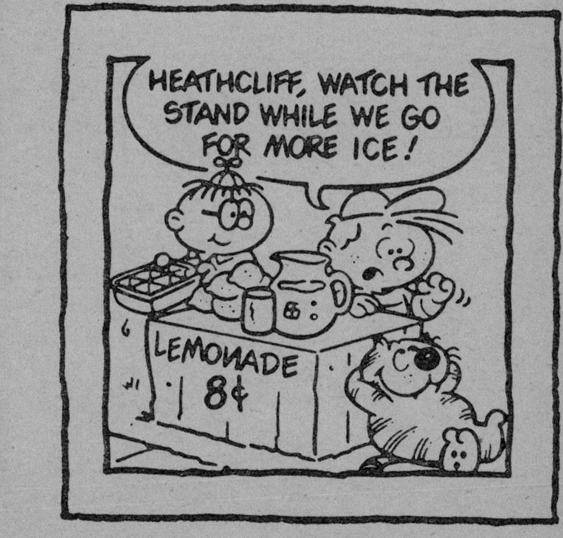
HEATHCLIFF, WATCH THE STAND WHILE WE GO FOR MORE ICE!
LEMONADE 8¢

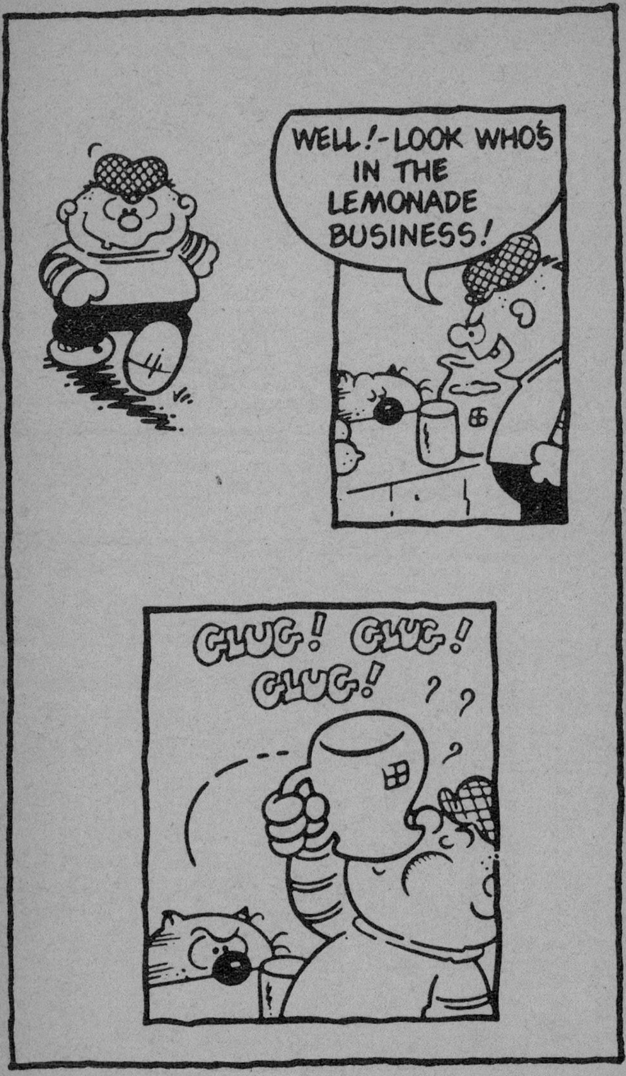
WELL!-LOOK WHO'S IN THE LEMONADE BUSINESS!
GLUG! GLUG! GLUG!
? ? ?

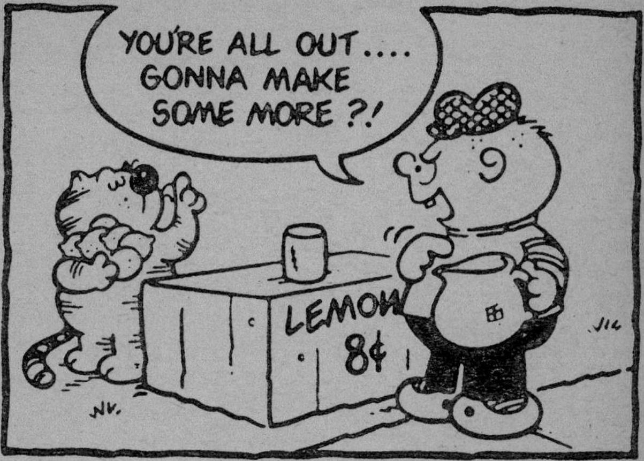
YOU'RE ALL OUT.... GONNA MAKE SOME MORE ?!
LEMON
8¢

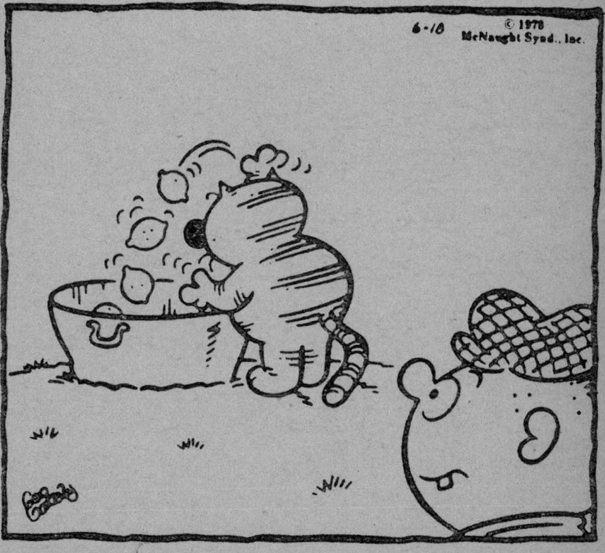
6-18 © 1978 McNaught Synd., Inc.

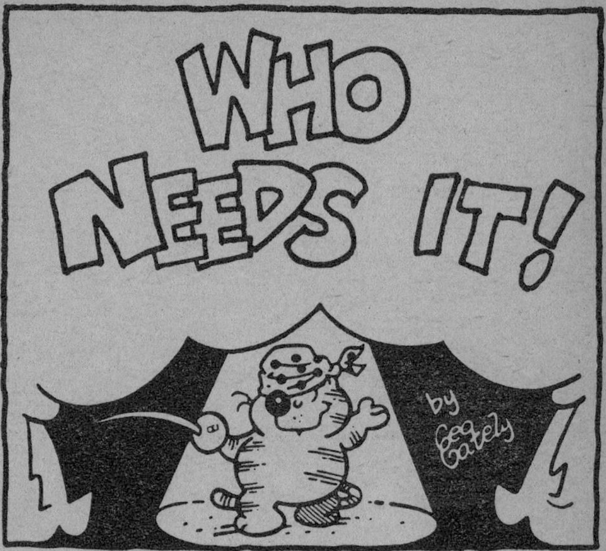
WHO NEEDS IT!

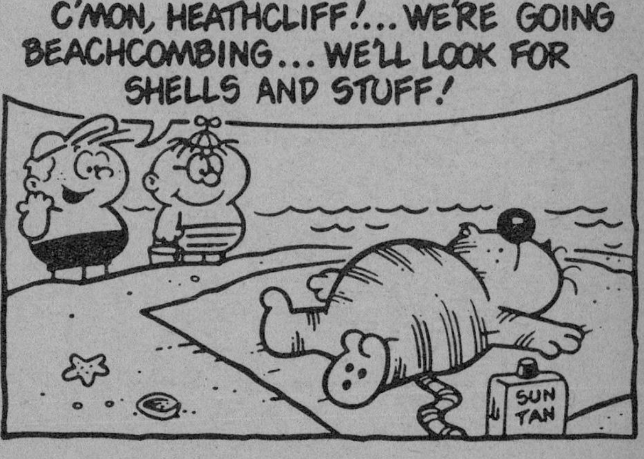
C'MON, HEATHCLIFF!... WE'RE GOING BEACHCOMBING... WE'LL LOOK FOR SHELLS AND STUFF!
SUN TAN

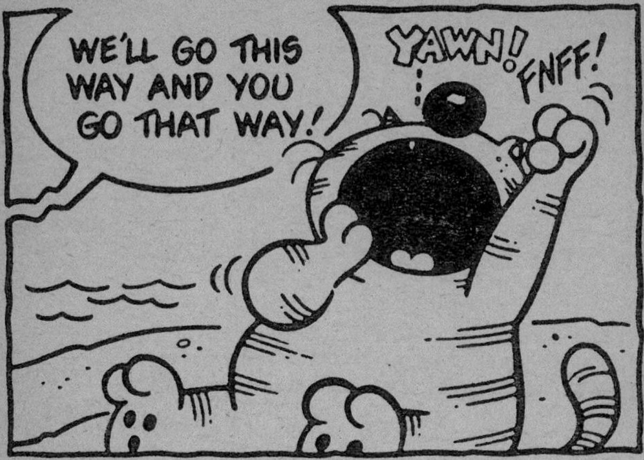
WE'LL GO THIS WAY AND YOU GO THAT WAY!
YAWN!
FNFF!

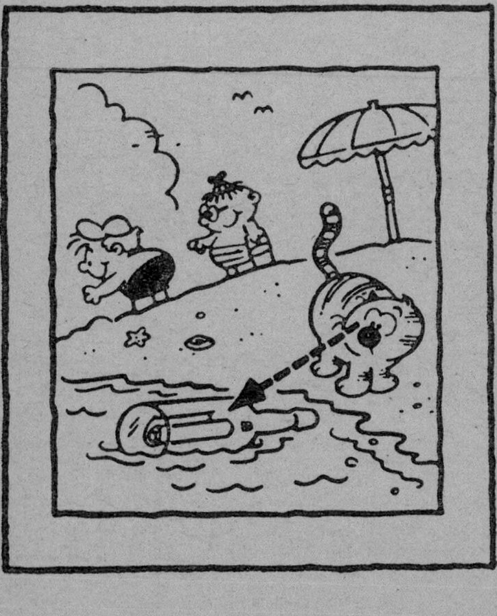

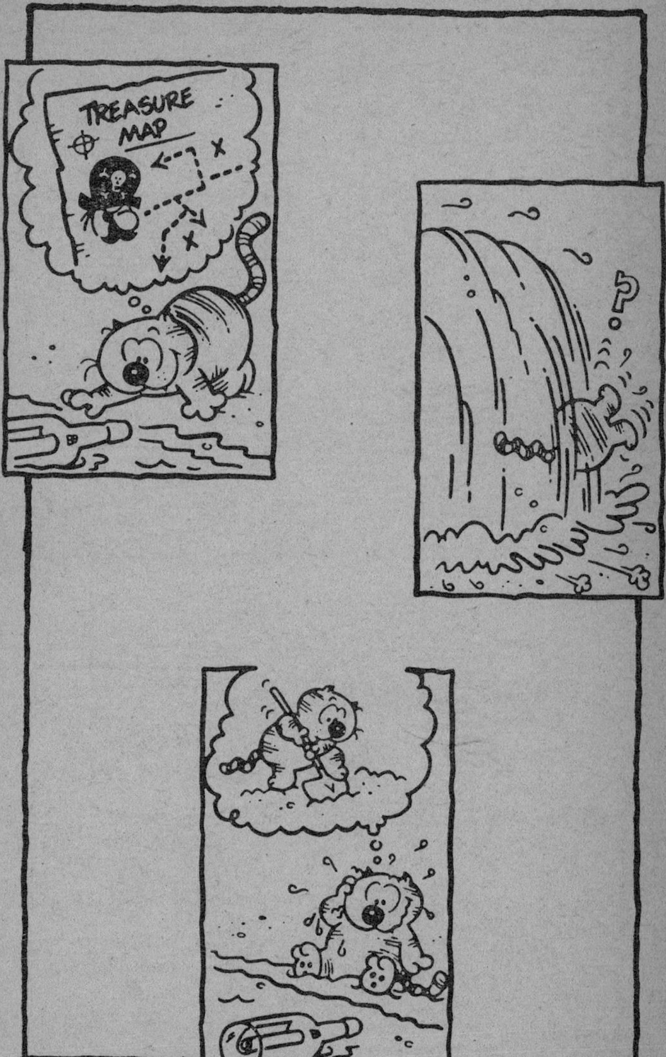
TREASURE
MAP

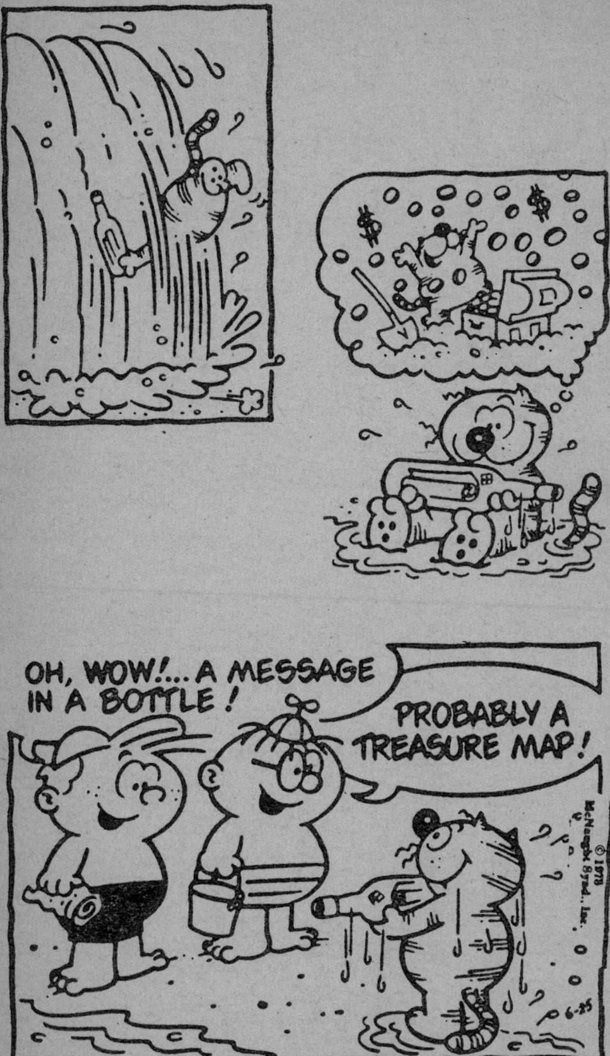
OH, WOW!... A MESSAGE IN A BOTTLE!
PROBABLY A TREASURE MAP!
© 1978 McNaught Synd., Inc.
6-25

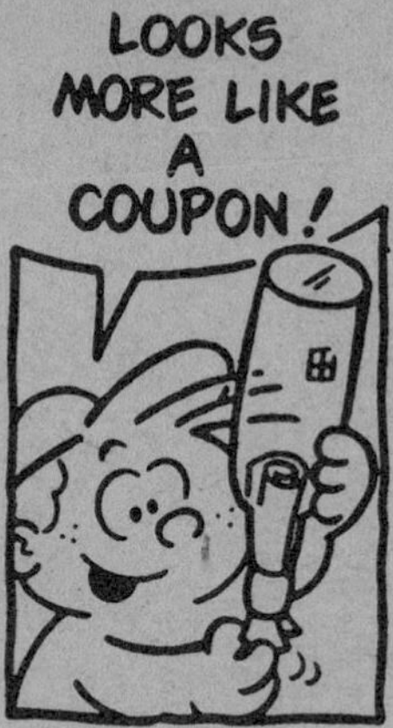
LOOKS MORE LIKE A COUPON!

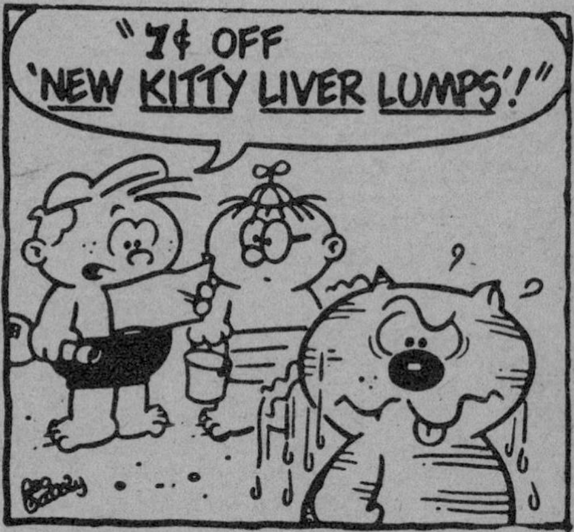
"7¢ OFF 'NEW KITTY LIVER LUMPS'!"

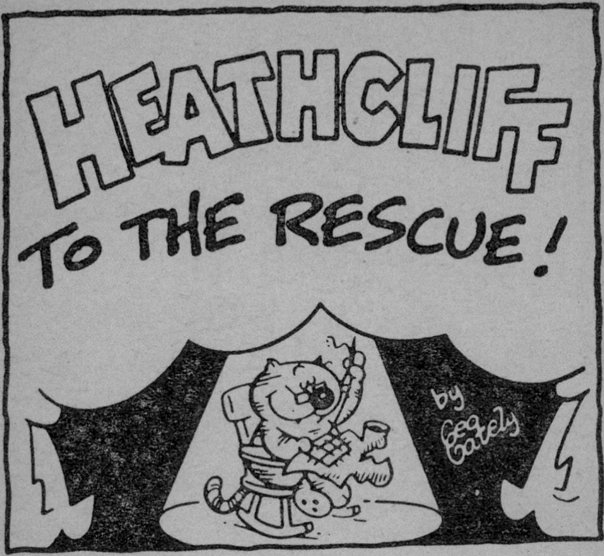
HEATHCLIFF
TO THE RESCUE!
by Geo Gately

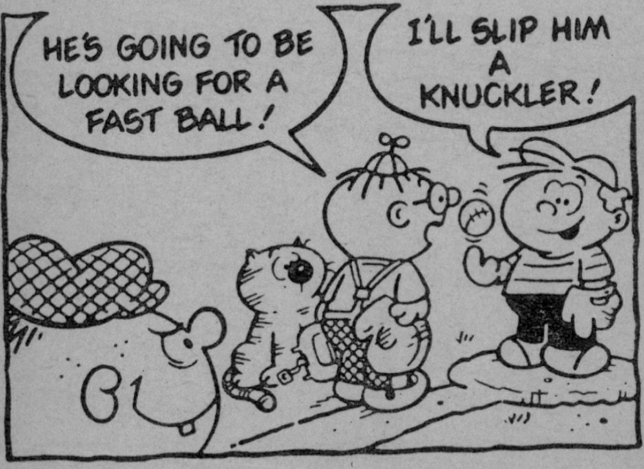
HE'S GOING TO BE LOOKING FOR A FAST BALL!
I'LL SLIP HIM A KNUCKLER!

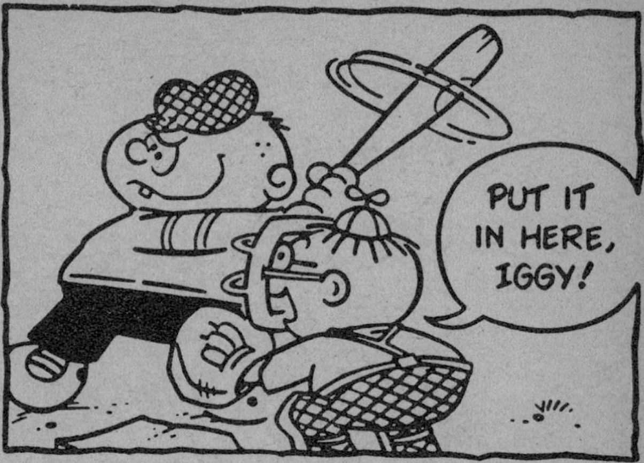
PUT IT IN HERE, IGGY!

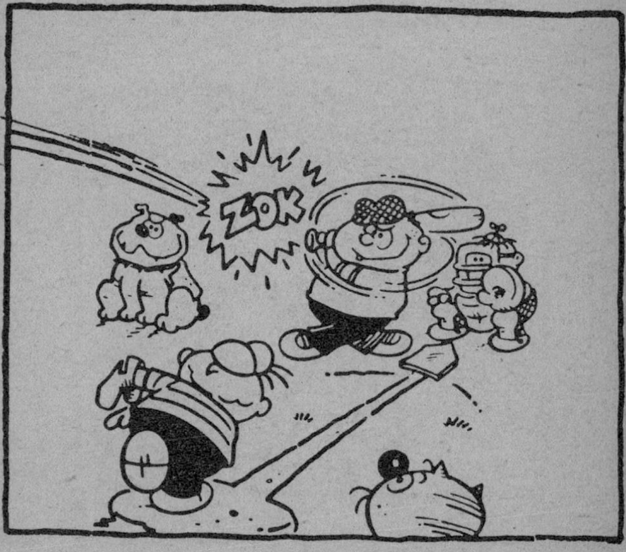
ZOK

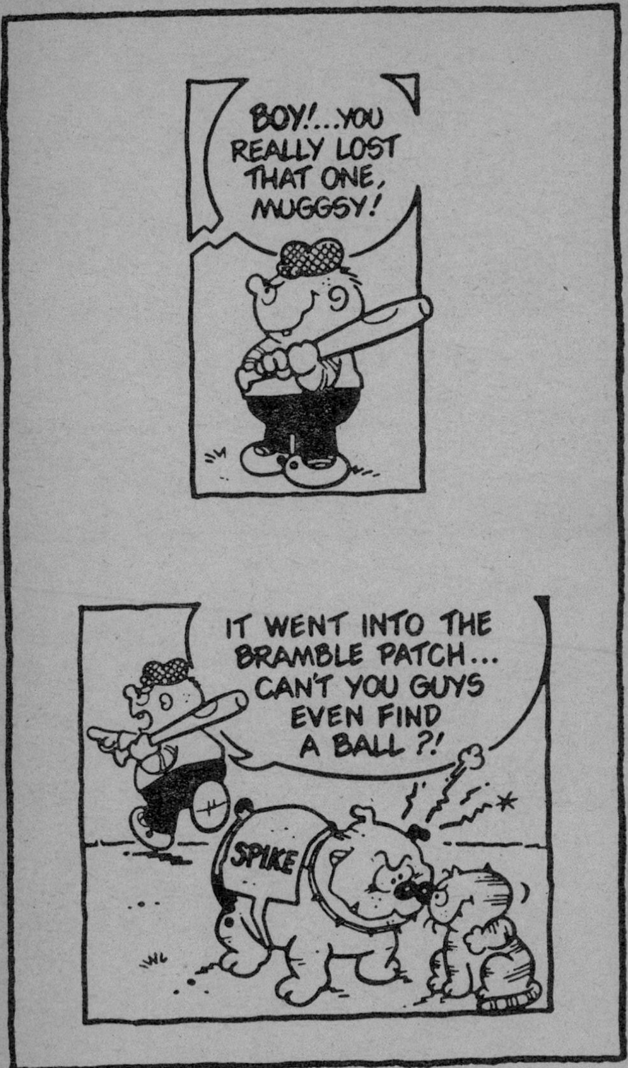
BOY!...YOU REALLY LOST THAT ONE, MUGGSY!
IT WENT INTO THE BRAMBLE PATCH... CAN'T YOU GUYS EVEN FIND A BALL ?!
SPIKE

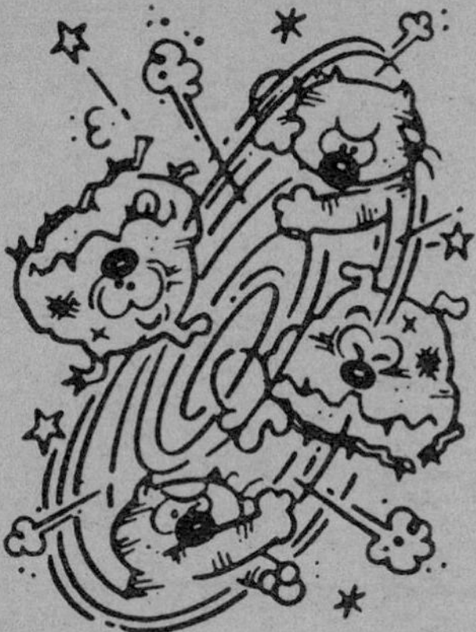

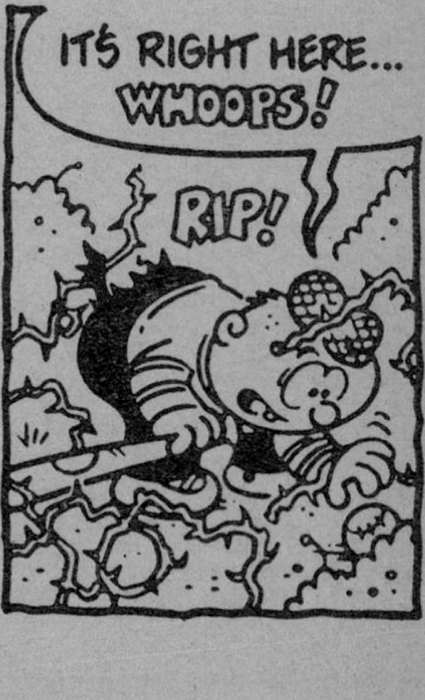
IT'S RIGHT HERE...
WHOOPS!
RIP!

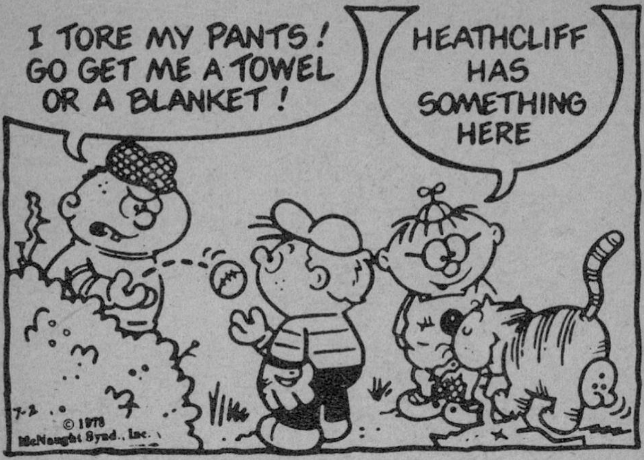
I TORE MY PANTS! GO GET ME A TOWEL OR A BLANKET!
HEATHCLIFF HAS SOMETHING HERE
7-2
© 1978 McNaught Synd., Inc.

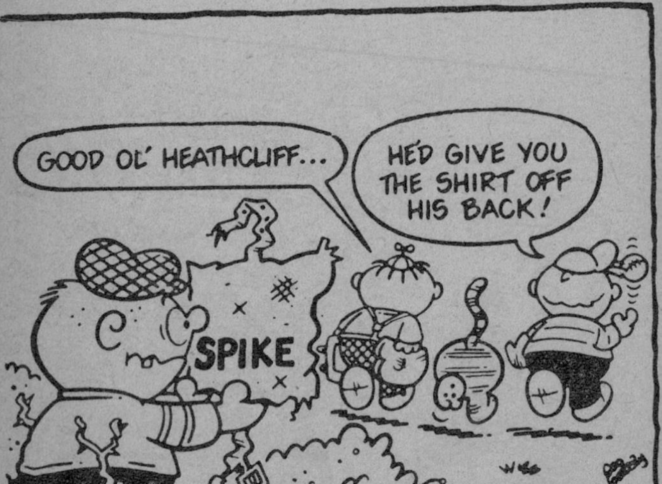
GOOD OL' HEATHCLIFF...
HE'D GIVE YOU THE SHIRT OFF HIS BACK!
SPIKE

FIRST OF THE MONTH AGAIN

by Gea Gately

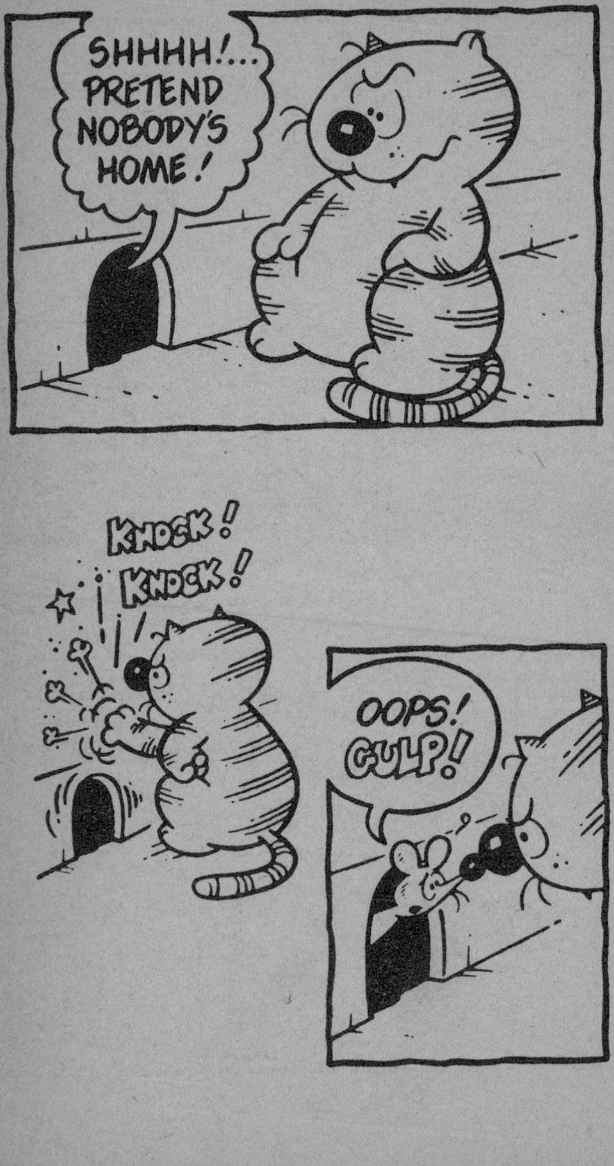
SHHHH!... PRETEND NOBODY'S HOME!
KNOCK! KNOCK!
OOPS! GULP!

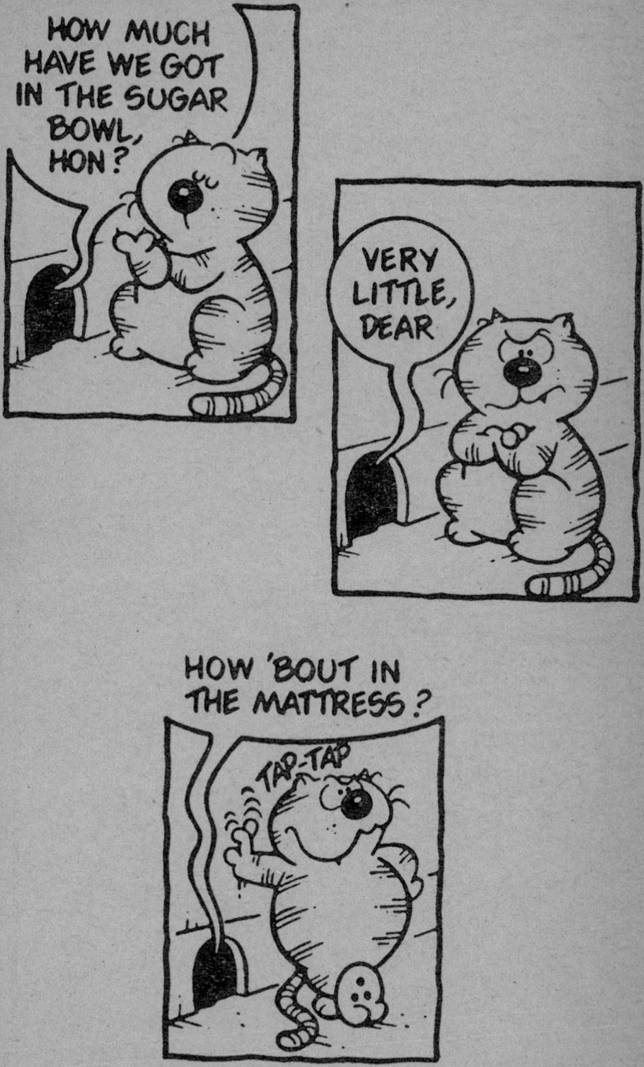
HOW MUCH HAVE WE GOT IN THE SUGAR BOWL, HON?
VERY LITTLE, DEAR
HOW 'BOUT IN THE MATTRESS?
TAP-TAP

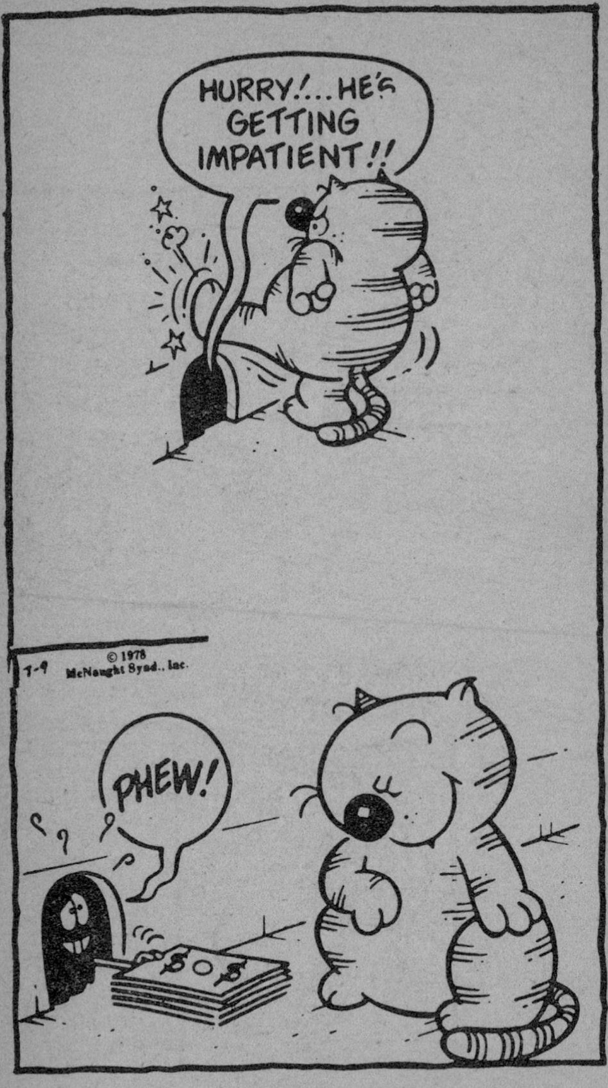
HURRY!...HE'S GETTING IMPATIENT!!
7-9
© 1978 McNaught Synd., Inc.
PHEW!

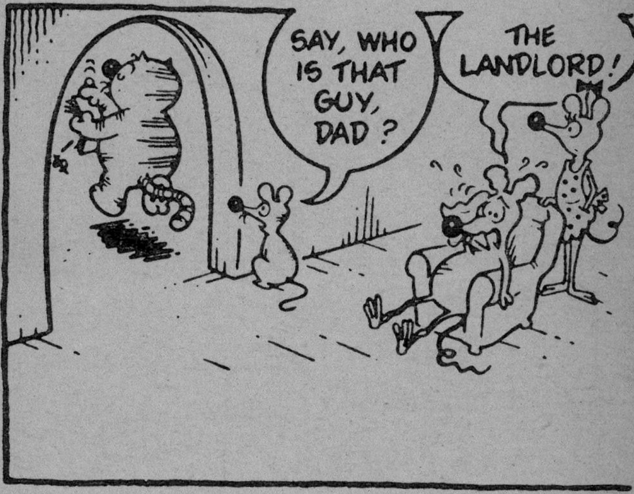
SAY, WHO IS THAT GUY, DAD ?
THE LANDLORD!

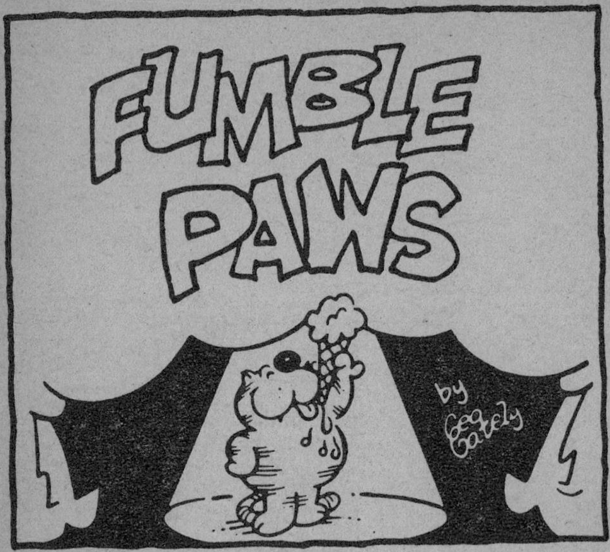
FUMBLE PAWS

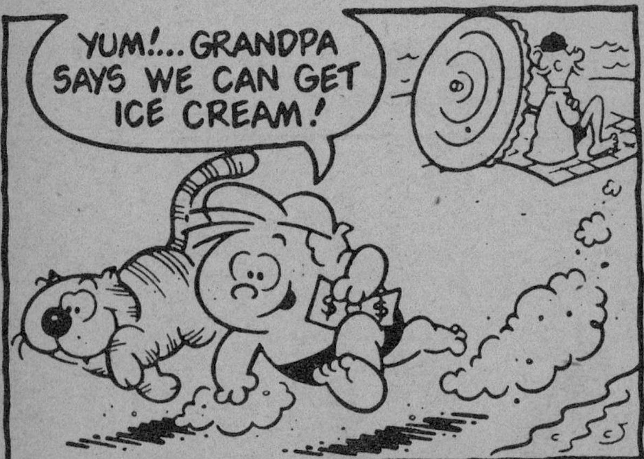
YUM!...GRANDPA SAYS WE CAN GET ICE CREAM!

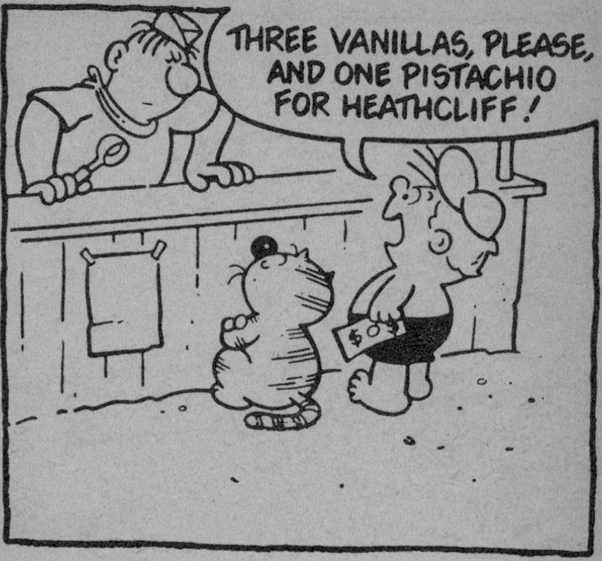
THREE VANILLAS, PLEASE, AND ONE PISTACHIO FOR HEATHCLIFF!

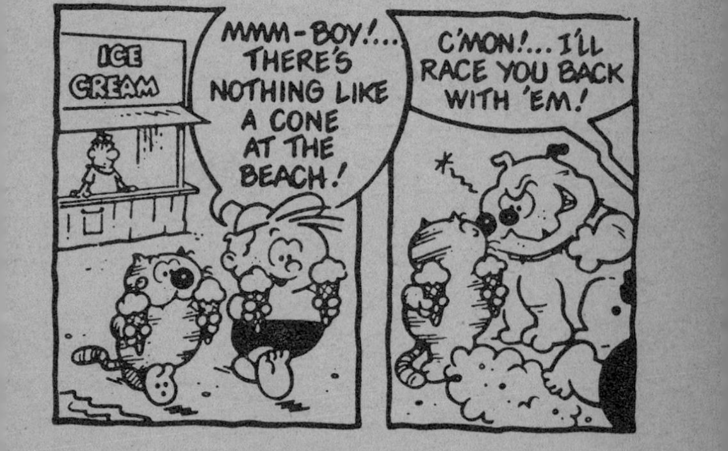
ICE CREAM
MMM-BOY!... THERE'S NOTHING LIKE A CONE AT THE BEACH!
C'MON!... I'LL RACE YOU BACK WITH 'EM!

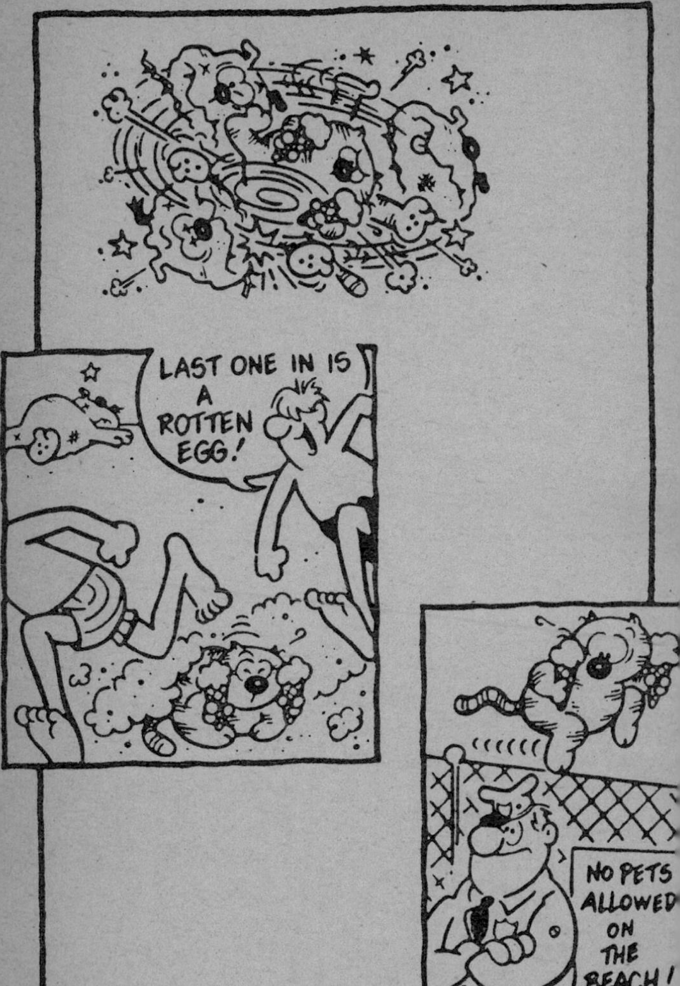
LAST ONE IN IS A ROTTEN EGG!
NO PETS ALLOWED ON THE BEACH!

© 1978
McNaught Synd. Inc.

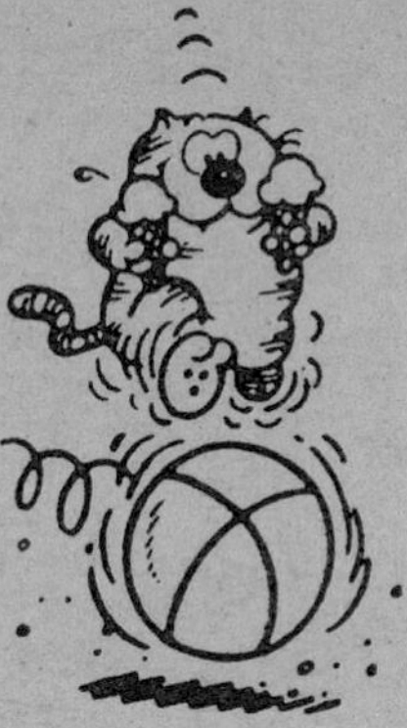

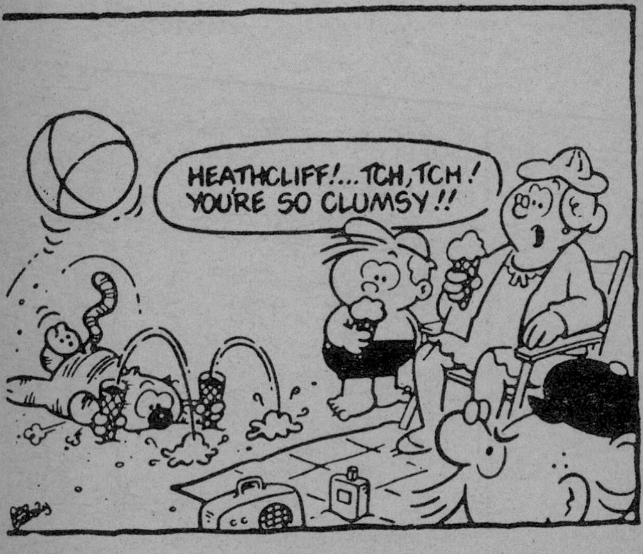
HEATHCLIFF!... TCH, TCH! YOU'RE SO CLUMSY!!

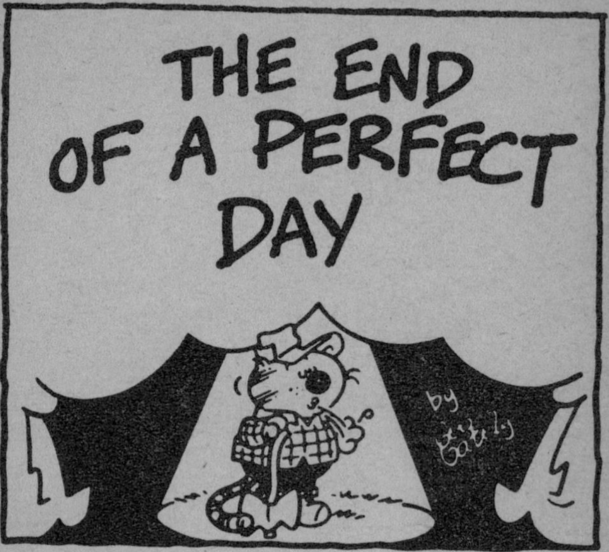
THE END OF A PERFECT DAY
by Gately

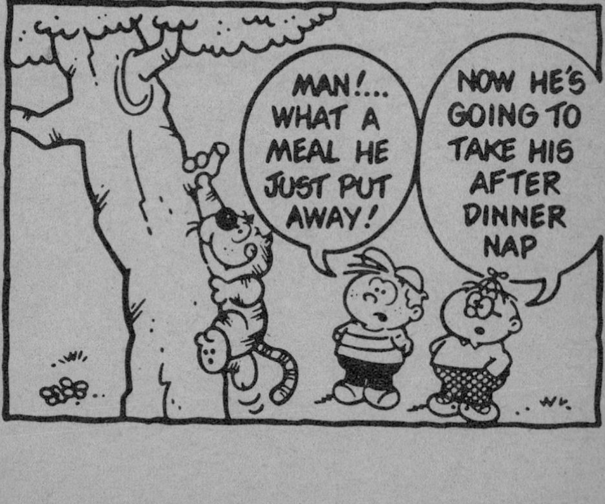
MAN!... WHAT A MEAL HE JUST PUT AWAY!
NOW HE'S GOING TO TAKE HIS AFTER DINNER NAP

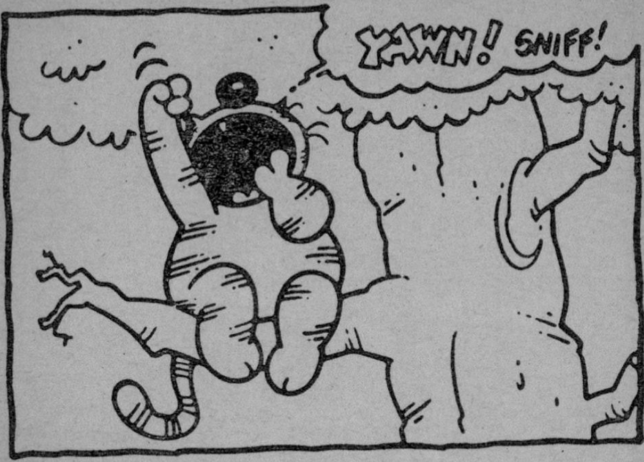
YAWN! SNIFF!

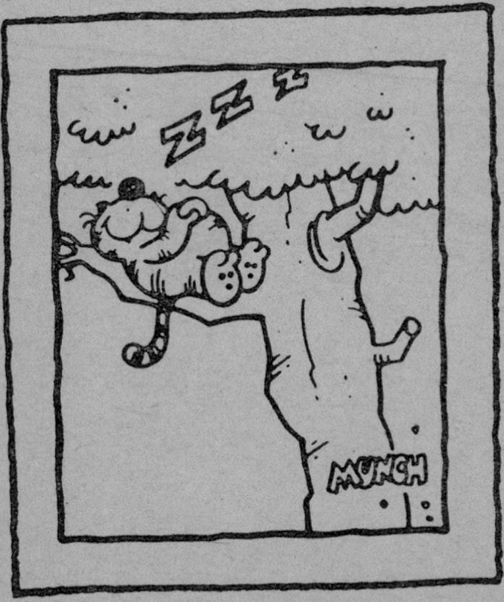
Z Z Z
MUNCH

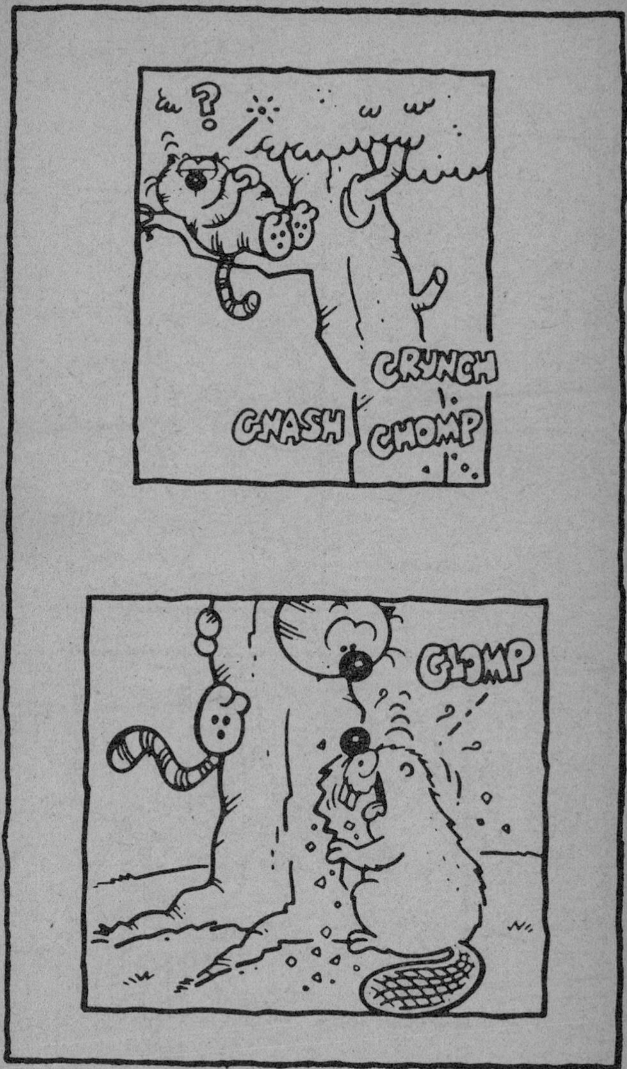
?
CRUNCH
GNASH
CHOMP
GLOMP

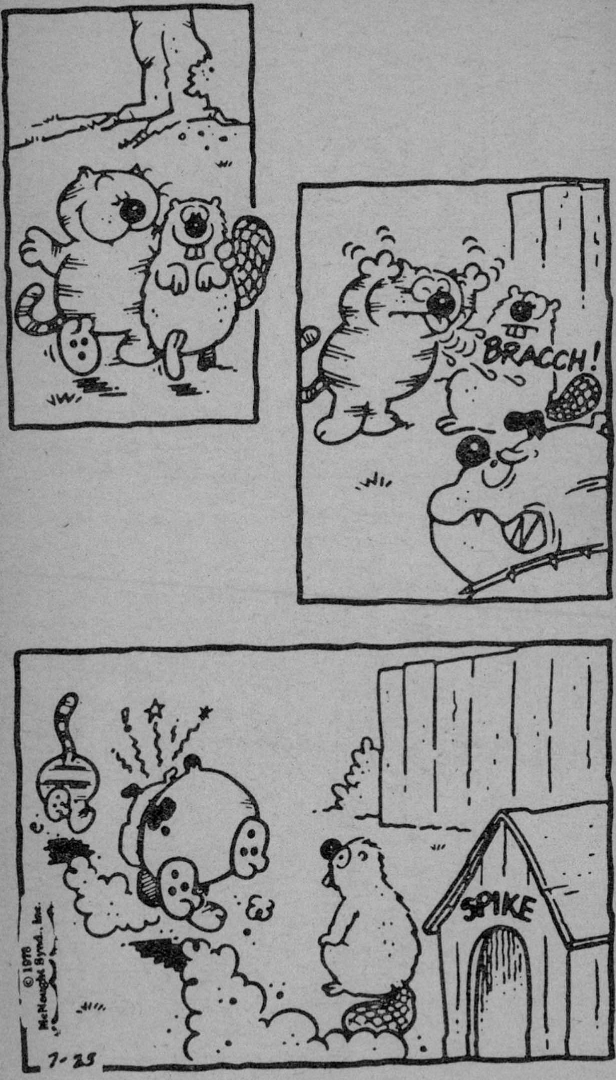
BRACCH!
SPIKE
© 1978 McNaught Synd., Inc.
7-23

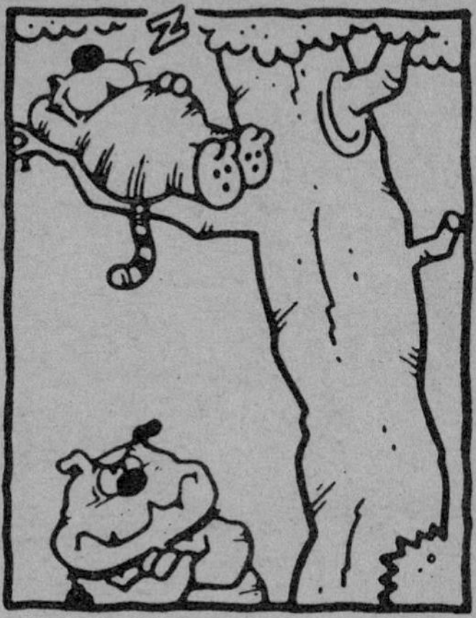
Z

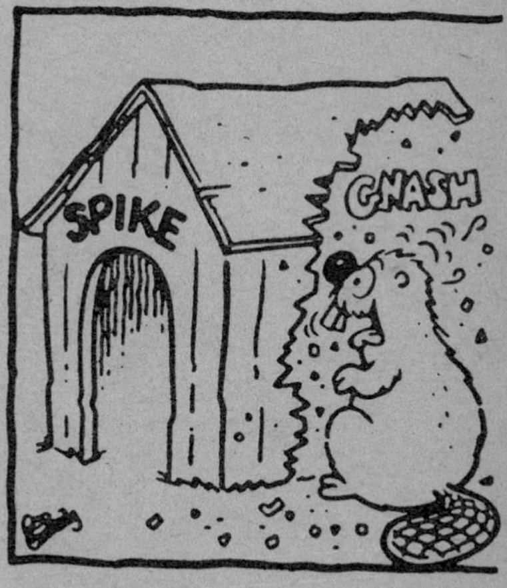
SPIKE
GNASH

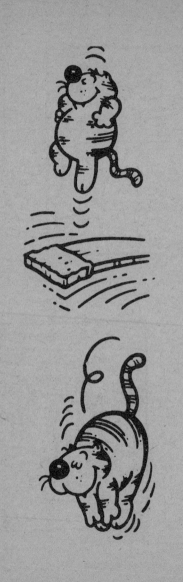

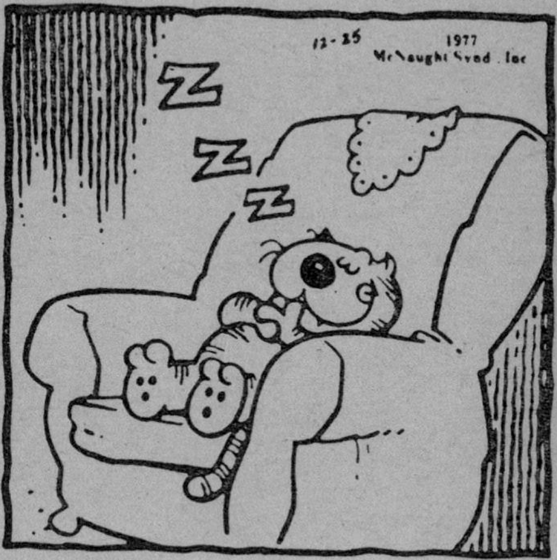
Z
Z
Z
12-25 1977
McNaught Synd., Inc

© McNaught Synd., Inc.

HEATHCLIFF

AMERICA'S CRAZIEST CAT

☐ 56800-1   SPECIALTIES ON THE HOUSE $1.95
    56801-X   Canada $2.50

☐ 56802-8   HEATHCLIFF AT HOME $1.95
    56803-6   Canada $2.50

☐ 56804-4   HEATHCLIFF AND THE $1.95
    56805-2   GOOD LIFE   Canada $2.50

☐ 56806-0   HEATHCLIFF: ONE, TWO, THREE $1.95
    56807-9   AND YOU'RE OUT   Canada $2.50

Buy them at your local bookstore or use this handy coupon:
Clip and mail this page with your order

TOR BOOKS—Reader Service Dept.
49 W. 24 Street, 9th Floor, New York, NY 10010

Please send me the book(s) I have checked above. I am
enclosing $_____ (please add $1.00 to cover postage
and handling). Send check or money order only—
no cash or C.O.D.'s.

Mr./Mrs./Miss _____

Address _____

City _____ State/Zip _____
Please allow six weeks for delivery. Prices subject to
change without notice.